The Forest's Silence

Silence

Book 6 of Adventures on Brad

by

Tao Wong

Copyright

This is a work of fiction. Names, characters, businesses, places, events and incidents are either the products of the author's imagination or used in a fictitious manner. Any resemblance to actual persons, living or dead, or actual events is purely coincidental.

This book is licensed for your personal enjoyment only. This book may not be re-sold or given away to other people. If you would like to share this book with another person, please purchase an additional copy for each recipient. If you're reading this book and did not purchase it, or it was not purchased for your use only, then please return to your favorite book retailer and purchase your own copy. Thank you for respecting the hard work of this author.

Books in the Adventures on Brad series

A Healer's Gift
An Adventurer's Heart
A Dungeon's Soul
The Arena's Call
The Adventurer's Bond
The Forest's Silence

Contents

Chapter 1

Daniel sat at the table on the second floor of a tavern, staring at the gate that once sent him and his party members into a Dungeon. A few weeks later, there were wooden barricades blocking exit from the entrance, and stone walls were fast forming behind those temporary barricades. Adventurers stood at attention behind the wooden barricades while even more city guards waited.

Daniel ran a hand through his black hair, his brown eyes tightening in memory over the last few weeks. The wooden barricades were the first thing to arrive, but soon after, the Adventurers Guild had started rotating Indigo and Violet teams to watch over the Dungeon entrance. Aided by the city guards, the goal was to stem any attacks that might arise.

"Anything?" Asin asked, her bestial growl erupting from her throat in a low purr. The Catkin sat down next to Daniel, long ears twitching as she peered out the window. Claws extended and retreated on her furry palms. Daniel looked away to meet Asin's violet eyes and shook his head.

"Do not worry. They are a strong team," Omrak said, sitting down. Yet, even the giant Northerner's usual good cheer was subdued, his words carrying little weight of conviction in them. In truth, no one held any further hope for the teams to exit the Dungeon. Too much time had passed. Food would have run out, and potions of healing and mana would be depleted. If they were still alive, any sensible team would have withdrawn.

Knowing that, the Adventurers Guild had taken action. It was their job to deal with Dungeons. Failure to do so meant that an outbreak would occur – especially in Artos. The Dungeon only appeared once in a while, allowing a small number of teams in before it shut down again. But now, it had appeared earlier than normal and had not been cleared. The Guild could no longer rely on past practice. And so, they watched and waited.

A thump next to Daniel took his attention away from the table. Tula set her plate of food down beside Daniel—the roasted vegetable, fresh bread and meat-filled stew setting his stomach rumbling. Daniel looked up, flashing Tula a quick smile. The Ranger returned the smile, her placid brown eyes given a sinister air from the small scar that bisected one eyebrow. "Don't mind me. Just had to grab a bite to eat when I smelled what they were cooking."

"I do not understand how you can eat that," Rob said, sniffing slightly. The Selkie's dark, oily hair caught the light as he joined the group, calloused hands cupping a mug of ale. "Their drinks are barely acceptable."

"Tastes fine to me," Tula said around a mouthful of food. "Eaten a lot worse on the road."

"Ugh. Rangers." Rob sniffed but then turned his gaze over to the window. "Any change?

Around them, the tavern buzzed with more business than it had seen in years. The tavern and the one across the street had become unofficial hangouts for many Adventurers with nothing better to do. A shared sense of loss and hope, of responsibility and burden, kept them close at hand in case the worse came to be. Yet…

"No." Daniel shook his head and gulped down a mouthful of beer. Rob was right—the beer here was barely acceptable. Nowhere as good as Erin's. But they did not come here for food.

"I was thinking we should try Portos next," Rob said, leaning forwards. "We're stalled on the fourth floor of Aramis right now, so we should do Portos. New monsters mean more experience. Might get us over the hump we need to level up."

"We've only run the fourth floor five times," Omrak rumbled. "It is insufficient to work out the proper methods to clear the floor. It only requires perseverance!"

"Sure, sure. I get that," Rob said. "But I'm just saying, we could run Portos and level up, make it down a couple of floors. Earn a little coin. Then tackle Aramis again in a better situation."

"I do not like giving up."

"Rob's not saying give up, just stop for a bit. And…" Tula paused and then ducked her head, sipping on the stew. Daniel cocked his head to the side, surprised that the Ranger had suddenly stopped talking. That was very strange.

"Ow!" Daniel exclaimed, glaring at Asin who had kicked him under the table. Still, he got the point. "What is it, Tula?"

"Nothing. Well, nothing right now…" Tula paused, visibly hesitant and then sighed. "But I got to go soon. In a week or so. There's a new expedition leaving Silverstone, and I've been requested to join it."

"What?" Daniel said.

"Luz's starry beard!" Omrak exclaimed.

"Oh…" Rob said.

"Yes. Sorry. Told you this was a short-term assignment. I've liked working with you all, really. But cities? It's not my thing, you know?" Tula said. "Rangers are meant to be in the forest. And this expedition is headed back towards my old village. Be nice to see my family again."

"That makes sense. Family is important," Daniel said, even as a flash of regret ran through him. He had none left now, making him just another adventuring orphan. There were a surprisingly large number of them. Or perhaps not so surprising when one considered the kind of job they took. It was easier to risk your life when you had nothing binding you close.

"Well, if you're leaving, that's all the more reason to do Portos!" Rob said, thumping his open hand on the table. "Otherwise Tula won't get the chance to see it. Or get the new monster experience."

That argument seemed to convince Omrak who rumbled his agreement. Asin just chuffed while Daniel scratched the side of his head, working out the timings. "When?"

"Tomorrow?"

"Can't do it. I promised time at the hospital," Daniel said, going over his own schedule. Since their successful run, Daniel had been flooded with offers to make use of his healing spells. Rather than constantly decline, Daniel had taken to working at one of Silverstone's hospitals part-time. There, he received a regular salary for his work, and the adventurers and Guilds were forced to pay the hospital direct. Since his schedule was publicly posted, the arguments over the use of his limited spells and Mana had dropped. It did not stop the invitations, but it had at least stemmed the flow somewhat.

"Fine. Day after," Rob said.

Murmured agreements broke out from around the table. Once that was done, Daniel started assigning roles to the party, ensuring that they worked together to not only stock and ready themselves for the new Dungeon but also gathered whatever information they could. After an agreement to meet again the next night to go over and plan the run, the group dissolved into cheerful bickering and reminiscing once more.

Yet, once in a while, one or the other of the party would look out the window, staring at the quiet Dungeon gate. Waiting.

Chapter 2

Portos was one of three Dungeons in Silverstone. One of two really since Artos was rarely open. Some newcomers, before the recent announcement, had not even known that Artos had existed. Because of the infrequency of Artos' openings, Portos and Aramis were the main Dungeons of the city, and the ones which had the greatest amount of information available. Aramis was considered the easier Dungeon. Its first three floors were an on-going repeat of the same form—flying imps and floating platforms. Dangerous if one was unlucky and careless but not deadly.

Portos, on the other hand, was not recommended for beginner Advanced Adventurers. It was not due to the dangerous terrain—though the dimly lit stone corridors were a pain to navigate and fight in. The issue that caused a problem was the demons that populated the catacombs. Each of the Zarask were lesser demons, known for their great strength and shriek ability. Even with earplugs in place, the shrieks were known to disorient fighters—forcing them to deal with the punishing strikes while still unstable. Too many Advanced Adventurers fell to such simple strikes, crushed underfoot, that the Guild had declared the first level only available to Advanced Adventurers coded yellow and above.

Daniel looked around the group one last time as they gathered outside the entrance to Portos. Seeing that everyone was there, the Healer raised his voice.

"Does everyone have their earplugs? Spares? Extra day's food and water? Spare pants and socks?" When everyone nodded, Daniel smiled. "Alright. Last time. Everyone, follow Tula's signs."

That was one of the other issues with going to Portos. Since earplugs were mandatory, teams had to learn a silent communication method. The vast majority of teams studied hand signals for that very reason. There were, in fact, three common types of hand signals—those taught by the Adventurers Guild, those in use by the army, and those used by the Rangers. Obviously, there was significant overlap among the hand signals, though the different groups often emphasized different aspects.

Together, the group followed along with Tula's hand signals and mouthed words, repeating after her with mostly fluid actions. After all, they had worked with the Ranger long enough to learn the basics—and had also studied further at the Guild.

"They're good," Tula said. Daniel smiled, touching the whistle that he kept under his shirt. If all else failed, they'd agreed on a single, sharp blast for a retreat. There were, of course, even more signals available via the metal whistle, but none of the team had learnt them. Or the light-based signals some other teams seemed to prefer.

"Let's go," Daniel said, waving everyone forward. As the group neared the guards watching over the gates, he ignored the knowing smiles of the guards, showing them instead his Adventurer card. He knew how silly they had looked, practising just before entry, but better silly than dead.

"Come," Omrak rumbled, clapping Daniel on the shoulder. "I shall lead."

"No. Mine," Tula said, rolling her eyes and good-naturedly shoving the big Northerner with her shoulder. The giant relented, stepping away and crossing his arms as the Ranger hopped through the swirling portal that led to the first floor of Portos. Still, the moment she cleared the Portal, the Northerner moved forwards, giving her a couple of seconds to clear the entrance before jumping through.

Daniel was next, his position in the middle of the group allowing the Healer to use both his heavier armor and shield as well as his healing ability to the maximum. Behind Daniel, Rob the Enchanter came. In one hand, the Enchanter carried his magical spikes, in his other, his newly purchased wand. Asin, their previous scout, was left to bring up the rear and watch their backs. Not that it was such a concern at the entrance, but still, it was good practice.

As Daniel stepped through the portal, clearing the entrance automatically with a little hop to the side, his eyes swept the Dungeon surroundings. Immediately, the Adventurer found himself vastly disappointed. Among other things, the Dungeon offered no grand vista or awe-inspiring sight, just another broken-down set of catacombs. Out one of the five doors that had been propped open, Daniel could see the dimly lit corridors that made up the first floor.

Dimly lit or not, the corridors still glowed with that low-level blue light that was a hallmark of the Mana-infused stone that was part of a Dungeon's environment. Daniel snorted, unhooking his enchanted warhammer and checking on the propped open door. Strange…

"Tula?" Daniel called out to the Ranger. She slunk over, flashing Daniel a frown for raising his voice in the Dungeon before she squatted down, eyeing the door. In a few moments, Asin joined the Ranger, and they began a whispered conversation consisting of single words, miming, and pointing. Daniel stepped back, taking guard behind the pair as he waited. In the end, it was Tula who looked up.

"Door safe. Doorway trapped. Magical," Tula said and then shrugged. "Rob?"

The Enchanter grumbled as he was finally called over. While he walked over, Asin carefully pried open the wood around the door jamb, showcasing the runic script behind. Rob squatted down, calling for more light, which was provided by Asin via an enchanted light coin before he fell silent, occasionally muttering. In the meantime,

Asin and Tula moved around the room, carefully checking the other doors and door jambs.

"Traps at the Dungeon entrance?" Omrak said, big arms crossed over his thinly armored chest. "That is unusual, is it not, friend Daniel?"

"It is," Daniel agreed. "I don't recall any of the other groups ever mentioning that as being common." In truth, while the Guild had books that were available for perusal, few Adventurers bothered checking the Guild records. Not only were the Guild records dry reading, but a large portion of Adventurers were also illiterate too. As such, the time-honored tradition of gossip supplied Adventuring teams with the vast majority of their knowledge about other Dungeons. "Asin, was this part of the records?"

Asin looked up and shook her head before turning back to the door. In time, the Catkin and Tula came back to Daniel, who continued to stand over the muttering Enchanter.

"No more traps," Tula said eventually. "Just that door."

"Why is this not recorded?" Daniel said, frowning as he stared back at the trapped door.

"That's because it's not a trap," Rob said as he stood up at last. "Also, it's not Dungeon-made. Even if it might look like it. And it's relatively new."

"How new?"

"Just about a day," Rob said, rubbing his chin. "I'm assuming the spiked doorway is to slow down the reclamation of the doorway by the Dungeon."

"What does it do?" Omrak asked.

"It's a location spell. The magical equivalent of a ball of string," Rob said. "There's also a warning signal to ensure that the Mage would be alerted if anyone walked through the door."

"Why not just use the floor?" Daniel said with a frown. It seemed to him that it made no sense to not only enchant the doorway but to hide that enchantment.

"Doorway because, if I'm reading the Mana flow correctly, the Dungeon will not fix it until the door closes. While a tile stone will begin its healing process almost immediately," Rob said. "As for the hiding…" Rob shrugged. "That I do not know. If Tula and Asin were not so paranoid, it is unlikely we would have seen the minor enchanting done."

Asin flashed a toothy grin at Rob's words, preening a little at the statement. While she did so, Daniel looked around the group and offered the team a choice. "Through this door or another?"

"It is a big floor. We should go in a different direction," Rob said immediately. "Whoever did this is obviously wary of others. Best not to cause trouble."

"More monsters in virgin territory," Omrak said, concurring. Asin nodded in agreement with Omrak, which gave them the majority. Of course, Daniel could have overridden their choice—but if he had meant to do so, he would never have even offered the choice.

"Alright. Earplugs then, everyone. Tula, pick a route."

The Ranger flashed a grind and nodded, heading immediately for another door set by itself on the south wall, directly behind the portal entrance. She examined the door again carefully before she pulled it open, an arrow already nocked in her bow. But, like the previous corridor, this one was empty and dimly lit.

With a wave of her hand, Tula led the group out of the safe area and into the Dungeon proper.

In silence, the group travelled down the dimly lit stone corridors, Tula padding ten meters ahead while the rest of the team followed. The Ranger moved slowly, scanning the floor, walls, and ceiling for hidden dangers. That this floor was known to host a couple of traps meant that even the impatient Omrak held back his impatience at their slow progress. As they approached their very first doorway, Tula slowed down even further, listening intently before creeping forward and crouching low to peer around the doorjamb. Once she was certain that no enemies lurked within, she waved the rest of them forward while she watched down the corridor.

Asin moved forward immediately, switching places with Rob, who kept watch for additional danger from behind while the Catkin entered the new room. This room was even more dimly lit, the Mana-imbued walls barely offering a glimmer of light. This was, of course, little hindrance to the Catkin whose eyes grew wide while drinking in the sparse light. Slinking within, her tail curled up close to her body, the black Catkin browsed the room, searching for trouble. Omrak stepped in behind her, stopping at the immediate entrance, ready to back Asin up if required.

The room itself hosted dusty shelves, broken pots, and a dining room table scarred with idle knife-drawn graffiti and a pair of abandoned plates. On the plates were the remnants of an old dinner, one covered with cobwebs like the corners of the room itself. Asin browsed through the room, doing her best to avoid touching the cobwebs and failing at times. Daniel had to hide a slight smile, seeing how the gossamer white spider webs clung to the Catkin's black fur. In a short while, Asin came out, holding a pair of copper coins. Daniel frowned slightly at the sight of the coins themselves, for their design was ancient and out of circulation. In fact, the coins themselves were slightly larger than the ones in current use. While Daniel had heard of the strange loot that Portos created, he still found the experience unsettling. What use was a Dungeon with abandoned, cobweb-filled rooms and ancient coins? Other than unnerving Adventurers that was.

Shaking off the thoughts and Panqua's strange perversions, Daniel waved the group onward. Tula immediately took off while the group prowled forwards. Twice more, the group stopped at abandoned rooms, coming out with another copper coin and a bar of sweet, unrotten cocoa. It was as they neared the third room that Tula brought her hand up, signalling the group to slow down. She slowly crept forwards while Omrak followed, unslinging his giant sword as he readied himself for the fight. Daniel drew a deep breath, pulling out his hammer and checking the straps on his shield once more while he waited. His iron-made plate armor was strong and offered him great protection, but it also made a lot of noise when he moved. His mediocre skill level in Stealth did not help at all.

Tula did her usual routine before pulling backwards slightly, removing her hand from the string of her bow and holding up her hand. Quickly, her fingers flashed while Daniel repeated the motions for those behind, just in case they missed them.

"Three enemies. One close to door. Two far away." Daniel paused, considering their options, and then he moved his own fingers, giving further orders. *"Asin up. I rearguard. Rob support."*

Once again the group rearranged themselves, mostly consisting of the two moving forwards while Daniel continued to hang back. On Tula's count, the group readied themselves before the Ranger stepped right past the doorway, drawing the arrow to her cheek and loosing in one smooth motion. The arrow glowed, small swirls of power gathering around the tip, as Tula triggered her Skill **Penetrating Arrow**. The weapon flashed, burying itself in an enemy. Even as Daniel watched, Omrak charged in with a shout, clashing with the closest monster, and Asin slunk in, offering ranged support with her knives.

A few seconds later, both Rob and Daniel began their approach towards the door. However, this approach and their team members' follow-up attacks were interrupted as the monsters unleashed their infamous attack and howled. The screams resounded within the small room, intensifying the attack before exiting into the stone corridors. Dust trembled and fell while the scream assaulted Daniel's ears, making his head hurt and his balance wobble.

On and on, the screams resounded before Asin and Tula managed to regain their footing. The pair loosed their area effect Skills **Arrow Storm** and **Fan of Knives**, multiplying their single arrow and knife into three or more of each. A short moment later, the screams cut-off, and the Adventuring team regained their footing. Rob quickly approached the doorway entrance, his wand glowing while Daniel watched the corridor for additional trouble.

Luckily, this time, no additional reinforcements arrived. In short order, the team managed to kill the Zarask, allowing Daniel to catch a quick glimpse of their attackers before they dispersed into blue light. Each Zarask was seven feet tall, and overly muscled with red skin and tiny horns that jutted from their heads. The Zarask bore two mouths—one on their head and a larger, elementally-infused mouth in their chest. It was from that mouth that the screams would erupt.

Once the bodies faded, Mana stones dropped from the creature's bodies, falling to the ground where Asin scooped them up. She handed one of the crystals to Rob, who slid it into a specifically designated pouch, before pocketing the other two. When the delve was over, they would pool the stones before turning them in for sale at the Adventurers Guild.

Once again, Daniel was struck by the strangeness of the Dungeon. Mana stones were the seed used by Erlis to remove the corruption that Ba'al spread through her veins. Dungeons were the areas which Erlis designated as the areas where she would push out the corruption. The stones themselves had a variety of uses since they contained Mana—the solidified lifeblood of Erlis herself. Still, more than one tavern-chair philosopher had deduced more efficient manners for Erlis to cleanse herself of Ba'al's corruption. It was, without doubt, quite inefficient to have

Adventurers enter Dungeons to cleanse the tainted monsters. And dangerous too when they failed.

It was only the temples that offered any real explanation, stressing that the Dungeons were a test, the grounds for the development of Erlis's children—humanity, the Beastkin, dwarves, and more. Of course, that raised questions about the importance of Adventurers and non-combat Classes, and of how Erlis felt about individuals who did not undertake the 'trial' of the Dungeon. To those questions and answers, Daniel was less certain. He knew that Priests offered generic platitudes—and that Adventurers and Dungeons were not the only way to gain Erlis' blessing— but…

It held true that experience, Erlis' blessing, was gained most prominently in the Dungeons.

***

Hour after hour, the Adventurers padded through the first floor of Portos. As the group left the safety of the original entrance, they encountered more and more Zarask. The large demons not only stood around within abandoned rooms but also patrolled the corridors of the catacombs, occasionally catching the team as they delved.

It was in the fifth hour of their delve that the team finally ran into their first true challenge. A patrol of four Zarask had turned the corner of a short corridor just as Tula had stepped out of her cover. Surprised, the Ranger had released her arrow by reflex, sinking the fletching deep in one monster's shoulder, but it was insufficient to stop the injured monster and another from screaming, staggering the group. While the team recovered and began to react, the other pair of Zarask demons charged Tula, engaging the Ranger in close combat.

Omrak charged and bowled over one such monster with his shoulder, using his Skill **Challenge of the North** to draw the attention of the other monsters. He then immediately fell back, wielding his greatsword in loops as he attempted to draw the monsters towards him.

Behind, Daniel charged forwards to back up the group. Unfortunately, Omrak, caught in his battle frenzy and unable to hear Daniel's approach, did not move aside to allow the healer to back him up. Daniel snarled, frustrated as he ducked and pressed himself into the left of Omrak, hoping to squeeze past as best he could. In the meantime, Omrak traded blows with the monsters, sword clashing with claws, and blood flying as badly blocked attacks flew. Unfortunately, the corridor was insufficiently wide to allow all the monsters to attack Omrak, and the slowest demon peeled away to focus its attention on Tula, who was still caught behind enemy lines.

Rob ran forwards, balls of enchanted ice held in his hand. The Enchanter ducked to the right, lobbing the two balls underhand. The balls fell forwards, triggering their payload between the feet of the red Zarask. Ice spikes exploded outwards, freezing and injuring the Zarask and slowing their progress, allowing Omrak to lop a limb off one. In the gap, Daniel finally found a space to push himself far enough forwards that he could spot Tula.

"Erlis's tears," Daniel swore, bashing a probing claw as he eyed the distance. Tula had dropped her bow, one arm hanging uselessly by her side while she wielded her large knife with her right hand to push back her attacker. But the Zarask had the advantage of reach and strength, each attack sending the smaller Ranger staggering. Drawing a deep breath, Daniel ducked down behind his shield as he peeked at his friend, drawing on his Mana to cast a **Minor Healing (II)** on Tula.

"Omrak!" Daniel shouted as loudly as he could, hoping the giant could hear him. Already, he could see the edges of red light glowing from Omrak's body as his rage ability triggered, giving the blond Northerner strength as he bled.

First, Daniel used a **Shield Bash,** slamming aside a claw strike. Then, he stepped forward and triggered **Double Strike,** bashing aside claws as he advanced. A blow staggered Daniel to the side, but he ignored it as he forced himself forwards, breathing heavily as his Stamina drained from repeated use of his Skills. Even so, he waded in and ducked close to his attacker, twisting his hips as he caught the Zarask along the torso with his knockback skill **Perrin's Blow**. The strike caught the monster and lifted it off its feet, sending it staggering into its caught and frozen friends.

The gap free, Daniel rushed forwards to help Tula. In the meantime, Omrak threw an overhand **Power Strike**, putting the full strength of his muscled body into the cut. Aided by his own passive **Lesser Strength** ability, the cut tore through chest and limbs, killing one monster. A second expired as Rob focused the floating spikes that he used as a defensive tool to plunge into its neck and back.

Even as Daniel reached Tula's attacker, a series of loud screams staggered Daniel from behind. Tula, caught unaware, missed a block and had her chest torn open. She flew backwards a foot before she slammed into the wall, slumping downwards unconscious.

Even as Daniel pushed himself to his feet, the Zarask spun towards the Adventurer, wide mouths hanging open, showcasing pink, wet skin. Screaming, the pair pounced at one another, exchanging blows. In the back of his mind, Daniel wondered where these new screams were coming from. And where Asin was.

Individually, these monsters were not that tough. While their special attack was annoying and their strength over-powering, Daniel knew he could win this fight. Better armor, better weapons, and more Skills were a powerful advantage. But in his haste to close in and finish the fight, Daniel missed a feint, dropping his shield too low and receiving the adjusted blow on the pauldrons of his armor. Daniel staggered low, a claw somehow having slipped between the plates and ripped into his shoulder, though the claw itself was left hanging.

On the ground, Daniel found himself staring in horror down the corridor that he had come from. There, Asin was struggling to keep a Zarask from crushing her while Rob crouched behind an Ice Wall that was slowly shattering beneath the attacks of another Zarask. Only Omrak seemed to be doing well, though he was hard-pressed by two demons. Forced into the corner, Omrak could not bring his sword to bear properly and was forced to grip his weapon in the middle of its blade, blocking and stabbing with both hands.

A foot appeared in Daniel's vision, moving quickly towards his face. The Adventurer tucked his head in tight to his chest, letting the blow catch the bottom of his chin and the helmet straps, feeling his body arch in pain. But the pain from kicking a metal plate slowed the demon down for a second. Long enough for Daniel to turn and crack the monster's knee, shattering it as **Perrin's Blow** forced the limb to move in one direction while the creature's weight moved in another.

As Daniel pushed himself to his feet, hesitating between going to save the injured Tula or joining the fight, Omrak yelled out loud. **Lightning Call**, the Northerner's defensive Skill, exploded from his body. Bolts of red lightning jumped from the Northerner to the two monsters near him, then jumped again to the still bodies, and again after that to Rob's attacker and Daniel. Pain engulfed those struck, teeth clenched tight, and Daniel's nose was invaded by the smell of burnt hair and crispy flesh.

Given a respite, Rob threw a series of small balls that struck and stuck to the Zarask's flesh. The balls then began to emit heat as they rotated, drilling into the heat resistant flesh of the monster. Resistant or not, the annoyance and the initial damage kept the monster off-balance long enough for Rob to control his floating defensive spikes to strike and injure the monster.

Omrak, having released his attack, lashed out with a foot and kicked a Zarask aside. Holding his sword up, the Northerner threw it like a shortened javelin, sinking the blade into the demon that fought Asin, allowing the Catkin to squirm away from the monster. At that point, Daniel finally regained control of his muscles, allowing him to strike the lower back of a recovering demon before Daniel turned and ran towards the injured Ranger.

A healer's instinct drove Daniel to do so, the **Minor Healing** spell flowing into his hand as he cast it on the Ranger before he reached her. This time the spell did even less, the gaping wound in her chest closing slightly before more blood pumped out. Lips pressed together, Daniel crouched over the woman, eyeing the unconscious Ranger.

Teeth gritted, Daniel slapped his hand down on her wound, pushing sliced guts back into place and rearranging broken ribs. Even as he did so, Daniel reached into his body, tapping into his Gift. An unlucky strike, a bad slip, and a critical hit had sent the Ranger to the brink of death. Basic healing potions and magic were little use, not when so much damage had been done. And so, Daniel did what only he could do.

Daniel reached into the Ranger's body with his Gift, finding the broken skin and damaged arteries, stitching blood vessels and muscles together. A wash of power from his **Minor Healing** went into the woman again, along with a **Healer's Mark**, but both were guided by his Gift. Fixing the most immediate damage slowed the death spiral, allowing his basic healing magic time to catch up and fix the rest. In seconds, the Ranger was stabilized, her wounds beginning to heal as Daniel kept her wounds pressed tight.

There was a price though. For miracles, there was always a price. The Gift was a curse to those who bore it. Each Gift by Erlis, randomly assigned it seemed at birth, also carried a price tag. A Champion might be forced to live with the pain of those who he commanded, bearing their wounds unseen. A Grandmaster Blacksmith might be unable to wield Mana at all. A Bard with a voice of the angels, unable to speak for weeks on end after using his voice. Or a Healer, who sacrificed his memories.

Mundane memories. Squatting in the forest as a child, grimacing as prickle berries lived up to their name as they exited. A campfire, late at night, waking to the sound of a wolf's howl in the distance. A howl that was answered by... something.

Other memories, less mundane and more important. The portion of a spell that he had been studying, fading away. An evening of drinking with a woman at the mining camps. Beautiful and brown-haired, a girl that he was sure he knew. Laughter. A shared smile.

Small memories. Big. They left in a rush as Daniel used his Gift. When he was certain his friend had stabilised, the healer released his grip on her with his Gift, allowing it to fall back into his body where it resided quietly. Waiting. Hungering.

"Is she okay?" Rob said, limping over. Somehow, somewhere, the Enchanter had picked up an injury to his thigh, though Daniel absently noted that he was not bleeding and was standing. Probably a bad bruise.

"She'll live," Daniel said, frowning. "She didn't manage to dodge. Tore her open." Daniel looked up, checking on the rest of his friends. He noted that they had survived the attack—both of his other friends sporting numerous minor cuts and, in Asin's case, a fast swelling lump over one eye. Daniel sighed, getting up and casually laying a hand on Rob's shoulder as he cast **Healer's Mark.** "Watch over her?"

"Of course," Rob said, taking Daniel's space. "Your skill is amazing. Seen a less serious wound kill before in my village."

"Just lucky," Daniel muttered, head ducked down as he refused to look at Rob as he walked away. Guilt washed over Daniel. Guilt that he had yet to tell his two teammates about his Gift. But, the danger of allowing others to know of the full extent of his abilities weighed on him. It scared Daniel, what the guilds, the kingdom would ask of him if they knew. So, he lied. And he healed his other friends.

Thirty minutes later, Tula finally woke up, her body mostly healed. It was still weak, the magical healing not being sufficient to bring her all the way to peak efficiency. Rather than risk another unfortunate encounter, the group retraced their steps, battling their way through random patrols before exiting the catacombs.

As they stood in the late afternoon sunlight, Tula looked over to the others with her pale face. "Sorry. I let you all down."

"Not at all, friend Tula," Omrak rumbled as he clapped the Ranger on the shoulder. This sent the little Ranger stumbling, only to be caught by Asin who hissed at Omrak. The Northerner blushed slightly but continued in his usual boisterous tone. "Any delve where one survives is a good delve. And we gained many Mana stones."

"Not as many as if we had gone with Artos," Rob said, crossing his arms.

"But we did get the new monster experience," Daniel said, contradicting Rob. "Which you wanted. And I got enough to level."

"Same," Asin concurred, flashing a wide grin.

Tula offered a weak grin, nodding that she too had managed to gain a level. Rob grumbled slightly, muttering something about missing a few hundred while Omrak shrugged. The large Northerner not levelling was not surprising—he had gone up only a few days ago.

"So, not a complete failure. Let's go turn in the Mana stones and the coins and then eat some food. You need lots of meat and proper rest. Tomorrow morning, I'll finish the healing," Daniel said, instructing Tula as the group moved off, considerably cheered.

As Omrak said—any delve where no one died was a good delve. At that thought, the group turned slightly, staring at where Artos was.

Yes. Any delve.

Chapter 3

The next morning, Daniel found himself lying in bed, a feeling of exhaustion and sluggish energy keeping him reclined. After the harrowing battle yesterday, he found that he could not achieve any significant level of motivation to leave his bed, especially knowing that there was nothing major that required his attention this day. No. Last night, he had roughly planned for a day of training and leveling.

At the least, Daniel thought, he could take care of his leveling. Focusing, Daniel called up the notification that sat in the corner of his vision, pulling forth the pronouncement from Erlis.

Level Up!
Adventurer Level 13
You have gained 5 attribute points.

Daniel sighed, staring at the meager gains. It was so true that gaining levels after one achieved the first ten was so much more difficult. It did not help that Daniel also had his secondary Miner class, forcing him to require even more experience than a single-class Adventurer. Not that there were many individuals who took Adventurer as their first class. Few people had the opportunity, never mind the desire.

Pushing those thoughts aside, Daniel turned to his character sheet. Perhaps Daniel's greatest frustration was the way his points had to be distributed. Unlike Omrak or Asin whose roles in the party were clear-cut, his was somewhat more nebulous. He was, of course, their Healer, but he also acted as a secondary front-line fighter. As a Healer, his Intelligence and Willpower ratings meant he could learn spells faster and cast more spells while regenerating at a higher rate. Though, with Mana pools filling once every six hours or so, that regeneration level was quite low.

That could be dealt with significant investments in Wisdom. Daniel knew of one Healer in the city who focused the vast majority of his attribute increases on Willpower. That meant he could cast a much larger number of healing spells than his brethren, allowing him to level up faster. Or so he claimed. The issue with that strategy was that at a certain point, Healer's needed to face and cure more and more difficult diseases to progress. Without investing in Intelligence, the ability to comprehend and cast the Mana-intensive medium and high-tier healing spells were significantly compromised. Then again, Daniel knew that Healer personally. Like many, he was content to spend his days working the basic spells and cures, again and again—after all, the vast majority of illnesses and injuries were repeats. Adventurers got cut, stabbed, crushed and impaled. It was rare that you saw high-level diseases or plagues. So, staying to low and mid-level spells made sense.

Of course, for Daniel, the issue was that he also needed to increase his three physical attributes as well. Initially, Daniel had a significant advantage in Strength due to his background as a Miner. Increasing his Agility made sense then to ensure he could hit his opponents. But now, splitting his level points meant that Daniel was fast becoming understrength for a front-line fighter. As an example, Daniel knew that Omrak had forty points in Strength and even more in Constitution. Only his Agility was lower, and that was not much lower than Daniel's. Asin on the other hand had—at last discussion—fifty in Agility alone, making the Catkin an extremely difficult opponent to pin down, speeding up the volume of her attacks. In contrast, Daniel's highest physical attribute was a thirty-two in Constitution—and that was his highest attribute.

In time, Daniel knew, if this kept going on with him splitting his attributes so widely, he would not be able to support on the front-line or as a Healer. It was time for Daniel to start seriously considering how he wanted to position himself in the team. While he could still hold his own in battle, the fourth level in both Dungeons were beginning to be Daniel's limit in one-on-one combat. To fix that, Daniel would need to spend more time on his hammer and shield techniques as well as gain another combat Skill.

Or… Daniel touched his coin purse. Perhaps there was another way around this. One of the side effects of being one of the few Healers in town was the high demand for his Skills. Even though he had not vigorously negotiated his salary from the hospital, he still earned a significant salary. Opening his purse, Daniel stared at the amount he owned.

In the pouch was just over sixty gold coins with scattered silver and copper. It was a veritable fortune. Enough for a family to live for five or so years. And he was still owed another dozen gold for the last week of work. With so many funds, there was no reason that Daniel could not upgrade his armor and equipment.

Clarity found, Daniel turned his attention to his attributes. As much as he was reluctant to embrace his role as a healer, it was, Daniel realised, a good cover as well for his Gift. The greater his expertise in 'normal' healing, the fewer questions there would be when he pulled off a miraculous healing. So long as he was able to hide his Gift in the shadow of his 'normal' healing, no one would likely drag him away from Adventuring. After all, while Healers were rare, Expert level teams all had at least one Healing-specialised member. It just was not viable otherwise.

Resolved, with only a slight qualm in his chest, one that Daniel pushed aside with the memory of a dying Tula, Daniel focused on his sheet once again and allocated his points. He split the points equally between Intelligence and Willpower, leaving the leftover point for Constitution. A dead Healer was a useless healer.

Once he had confirmed his attributes, Daniel next turned to the numerous notifications about skill gains he had been ignoring. Since the skill development occurred whether or not Daniel read the notifications, the Adventurer often took his time reading over the information before planning out his training strategies to optimise his development. Right now, there were a few notifications that were particularly interesting.

Skill Level Up

Club Skill has increased to Novice 8 level. +9% damage for all club-based weapons.

Skill Level Up

Shield Skill has increased to Novice 7 level. +8.5% damage mitigation for all shield blocks. +4.25% for damage done using the shield.

Skill Level Up

Combat Sense has increased to Novice 5 level. Increased awareness of enemies and allies gained. Increased perception of damage dealt and received. Increased combat flow.
New Skill Proficiency Available.

Skill Level Up

Healing Skill has increased to Novice 5 level. +7.5% increase in damage healed via magical and non-magical means. +3.75% increase in non-magical healing speed of those treated.
New Skill Proficiency Available. New Spell available.

The healing skill increase was particularly interesting. While Daniel had received new spell options before, this was the first time he had achieved the option of a skill proficiency. For a moment, Daniel daydreamed of the type available before he pushed the thought aside. There was nothing to be done about it until he gained his next level. Rather, Daniel pulled up his new status to admire the changes in his body since the last time he viewed his sheet.

Name: Daniel Chai (Advanced Adventurer)	Race: Human (Male)
Chai Rank	
Class: Level 13 Adventurer (0.9%)	Sub-classes: Level 7 (Miner) (2.4%)
Life: 343	Stamina: 343
Mana: 257	

Attributes

Strength: 29	Agility: 25
Constitution: 33	Intelligence: 29
Willpower: 23	Luck: 17

Skills

Unarmed Combat: Level 8 (94/100)

Clubs (Novice): Level 8 (32/100)

Archery: Level 3 (24/100)

Shield (Novice): Level 7 (14/100)

Dodge (Novice): Level 3 (21/100)

Combat Sense (Novice): Level 5 (14/100)

Perception (Novice): Level 3 (77/100)

Mining: Level 7 (58/100)

Healing (Novice): Level 5 (13/100)

Herb Lore: Level 3 (98/100)

Stealth: Level 2 (42/100)

Cooking: Level 4 (18/100)

Singing: Level 2 (14/100)

Tactics: Level 4 (12/100)

Skill Proficiencies

Double Strike

Shield Bash

Perin's Blow

Find Weakness

Mapping (II)

Inventory (Adventurer Special)

Spells

Minor Healing (II)

Healer's Mark (I)

Gifts

Martyr's Touch—The caster may heal oneself or others by touch and concentration, sacrificing a portion of his life to do so. Cost varies depending on the extent of the injuries healed.

Invigorated by the changes, Daniel swung his feet off the bed and quickly washed up. Downstairs, he found that his team had already split off except for Tula. A quick healing ensured that his teammate was back to top form.

"Got to report in," Tula informed Daniel as she waved goodbye and skipped out of the inn.

Daniel, alone, sat down to enjoy a slow breakfast. Better to do that now and then go shopping as per his newly resolved resolution. Since all his weapons and equipment were stored in his Inventory, Daniel was certain he could visit the various merchants and, if necessary, get his equipment directly enchanted. Though…

"I wonder if Rob could do it?" Daniel said, tapping his lips. Definitely something to consider. After all, the Enchanter might be low-levelled, but Daniel might be able to gain a cheaper enchantment that way. Of course, Daniel would pay. But it was interesting that Rob had yet to offer. Perhaps the Selkie thought that it would intrude on the team? Or that his ability was not sufficient?

It was true that Rob was still relatively low-level like the rest of the team. Still, it was worth looking into when he next met up with the man. Humming to himself absently, Daniel quickly finished his breakfast, thanking the smiling innkeeper before he left.

***

Another advantage of being a healer was the ability to acquire reliable knowledge quickly and easily. While the majority of the work that Daniel did at the hospital was more serious, most ailments that were treated at the large building were less than life-threatening. In fact, most of the work Daniel did was less than life-threatening. As such, gossip and news travelled through the hospital at a decent clip. Which meant that it took only one brief stop before Daniel was on his way with three names under his belt.

Daniel's first stop was to a well-known armourer who dabbled in enchantment. Unfortunately, the armourer flatly refused to work on Daniel's existing iron plate armor, nearly spitting in fury at being asked to sully his work on 'slipshod, orc-manufactured trash'. Feeling somewhat insulted, like his armor, Daniel left to visit the next on the list. This blacksmith specialised in weaponry, but after taking a look at Daniel's enchanted warhammer, he explained that he could offer little additional help. He did then try to sell Daniel on a host of other weapons, one of which Daniel was secretly desiring.

Ifrit Dagger of the Third Flame

Effect: The Dagger of the Third Flame is enchanted to wrap the dagger in flame. This weapon will cause fire

---

and burn damage (20-30 points) when in contact with targets.
  Durability: 50/50
  Item Class: Enchanted
  Quality: Excellent (+5 to Enchantment Damage)

Rather than purchase the item on impulse, Daniel put the decision aside until he had visited the last shop. The weapon itself was significantly more powerful than the bracers that Daniel had once worn, but the bracers had been made for a Beginner Adventurer after all. They also had the advantage of enchanting Daniel's aura which meant that all his strikes had been enchanted. This weapon on the other hand was the only item enchanted.

As Daniel walked down the street, the Adventurer paid careful attention to passersby. Even now, months after arriving, Daniel still found the sheer size of the city intimidating. Since Daniel had spent the vast majority of his life moving from mine-to-mine as each played out, he had rarely visited the cities that abutted the mountains he had worked at. Only occasional trips with his grandfather had provided Daniel the context he needed to not be completely overwhelmed. It did not help that the shops that held enchanted goods were all based in the richer, more prosperous quarters of the city. So, it was with some relief that Daniel finally found himself at the entrance to the last shop. The store itself even had glass windows, the mostly clear glass a testament to how prosperous the Enchanter who stayed within was. Showcased in the shop window were numerous accessories, ranging from necklaces and earrings to the ever-popular rings.

Inside the shop, a smiling female attendant with dimples and auburn hair greeted Daniel cheerfully. Yet, for all her smiles, Daniel noted the way she gave the Adventurer a quick once over, her gaze lingering on his belted warhammer.

"How may I help you, Adventurer?"

"Daniel," he said, introducing himself as he walked forwards. "I'm looking for, well, enchanted accessories." Realising how inane that sounded considering where he was, Daniel rushed on. "I have a problem. I need to start doing more damage, but I can't put many points into my physical attributes."

"Kaylee," the attendant said, touching her chest. "And that's an interesting problem. I have a few thoughts, but if you could explain a little more?"

"Of course," Daniel said and then paused. "Umm, I don't want to be rude, but are you the Enchanter? Just that you're a little uhh…"

"Young?" Kaylee's smile didn't move an inch.

"Pretty," Daniel said, trying to recover from his gaffe. Then, realising what he said, he blushed even further and coughed.

Kaylee said nothing to his rude response, though her eyes grew a little colder as she spoke. "I am a seventeenth level Enchanter. The work here is both mine, my fellow apprentices, and my Master's. Today is my turn to watch the shop."

"Right. Sorry," Daniel said, scratching his head and offering the woman a half-smile. Kaylee just gestured, and Daniel took a breath, exhaling slowly as he thought of what to say. "I'm a healer. I used to fight on the frontlines. Well, I still do. But I need to hit harder. And be a little better defended. Not much. I'm a plate and shield user."

"I see," Kaylee said, glancing over Daniel once more. "Is there a reason why you haven't purchased enchanted defenses?"

"Well, not really," Daniel said. "I just thought of this now. Or well, had the funds for it now. And I'm in a bit of a rush for an upgrade. And a full suit is both expensive and time-consuming."

Kaylee could only nod at that. They both knew that enchanting a full suit of plate mail would be extremely expensive. Instead, Kaylee tapped her lips with one finger, beginning to chew on a fingernail in thought before she pulled it out of her mouth with a jerk. The saleswoman eyed Daniel and seeing that he saw her entire action flushed slightly.

"Sounds like our accessories are the best option then. Your hammer will be sufficient for now, though it'll need to be upgraded in a few levels," Kaylee said. "But we can put that off with the right accessory. Now, do you know much about enchantments?"

Daniel shook his head, and Kaylee smiled slightly. "That's good actually. Most Adventurers think they know, and then they end up making mistakes later. Better to get a proper education."

"Okay."

"Now, let's start with the basics. The first type of enchantment is a material enchantment. It magnifies and reinforces the properties of a material. A lot of enchantments are of that kind because they're the easiest to make. Not necessarily cheapest—because the material can be expensive—but the easiest. That's where you get weapons like fire-toothed daggers or ice claw sabers." Daniel nodded, recalling seeing such weapons at the other shop. "But they're uncommon to make and have lousy durability."

"The second kind of enchantment are spell-driven enchantments. Your warhammer is one. In such cases, a spell is enchanted into the weapon itself. Those are more complicated to make because you can only enchant a spell that you know—or that you can have a mage cast at the time of enchantment. That's why they're often either very common—like a flame or ice-based weapon—or extremely rare. Not much in-between."

"Oh," Daniel said, touching his warhammer. "Are spells like the imprisonment one I have that common?" Or did he have something super-rare.

"No. Cage spells are common enough, but to keep one inside a weapon for an unknown period of time…" Kaylee's lips quirked slightly. "No. Not at all. It's a Dungeon drop, no?" At Daniel's nod, Kaylee smiled slightly as her voice firmed. "Dungeon weapons are different from those we create. Spells that are stored for use and re-use have three components. First, the recharge portion. Complicated, difficult to make, and often dependent on the materials. Second, the spell itself. The more powerful the spell, the more powerful the third component needs to be. The container for it.

"All three of these must be balanced by the enchanter—and finding and developing the balance is what makes higher level Enchanters better. But, Dungeon weapons alter the equation slightly by altering what is considered a 'powerful' spell. While I can—and do—replicate the first and third components easily, the spell itself is a divine spell. A low-level divine spell. But a divine spell nonetheless."

"Oh…" Daniel said softly, touching the weapon unconsciously. He had never realised his weapon had been that powerful. It seemed strange that such a powerful spell would be on such a— relatively speaking—poor weapon. But then again, as Kaylee mentioned, its ultimate maker was

Panqua. What a god viewed as powerful or not was unlikely to be the same as Adventurers like themselves.

"Good. Now, we were talking about types of enchantments. The first material, the second spell. The third are glyphed spells. Rather than enchanting and storing a spell, the enchanted effects come directly from the glyphs themselves. Of course, I say glyphs, but there are a variety of different cultural practices that use everything from runes to glyphs to hieroglyphics. The effects in the end are the same. The glyphs draw from the ambient Mana, charging up the enchantment, which, in turn, exhibit the effect. The major difference is that in a glyphed enchantment, nothing is actually stored—the Mana is converted immediately."

Daniel frowned. "I understand the glyphed spells, but what umm, do they do?"

"The most common kind are those that directly affect one's aura," Kaylee said. She waved Daniel over to a case, even as his face started clearing up. After all, he had direct experience with an enchantment like that.

"See here? These rings on the top are all glyphed rings. They're mostly aura-enhancers— with the gems giving an indication of the kind of enhancement to your aura. So, blue for cold, red for fire, white for holy, black for energy drain," Kaylee explained. "We do recommend that you don't wear them outside of the Dungeon of course."

"I had a bracer that enhanced auras," Daniel interjected. "Couldn't wear it underneath my current armor."

"Well, that's why we prefer accessories," Kaylee said with a smile. "Now, the second line down are the spell-woven ones. These hold and contain spells, with the knotwork around the stones indicating they are spell-woven."

"That's smart," Daniel said, understanding how the simple design difference would make the type quite clear.

Kaylee preened at Daniel's words a little, brown eyes dancing as she added, "Now, the stones are the same, but most of our spell-woven rings are projectile-based. Popular among our mages since they don't require gloves. It allows them to deal additional damage that's not reliant on their own Mana. But I wouldn't necessarily recommend that for you."

Daniel nodded, not really desiring a lower-powered spell version of a Mage's firebolt. "And the third type, the material-woven rings are below." Statement, not a question, since those rings were not bands of steel or gold, but were instead fewer in number and stranger in variety. There was a stone-chiselled ring, at least three that looked to be made of different kinds of bone, another that seemed to be a hollowed-out finger ring, and another that seemed to be made of dried skin.

"Yes. Those are our Master's specialty items," Kaylee said proudly. "The ring of greater life drain," a finger pointed to the hollowed finger-ring, "is probably the most effective enchantment for dealing damage. So long as your opponent is living and is hit, you'll be guaranteed to steal five percent of their life. And gain about ten percent of what was drained to your own health."

Daniel eyes widened, then narrowed as his healer's knowledge went to work on trying to picture how that would work. It was likely a mass regeneration effect like most health potions—increasing the speed of healing in a body indiscriminately, with maybe a slice of energy gifting as well. It was nice, but dangerous to overuse in certain circumstances. Misaligned bones, punctured organs and the like could cause significant issues in the healing process.

"Even then. That's amazing," Daniel said. A five percent guaranteed damage of life was significant. But, not surprisingly, the enchanted ring was also priced for its effectiveness. Daniel shook his head, discarding any idea of buying the ring. Even if he gathered all the funds he had ever earned, he would still not even be close to achieving the necessary amount. "I don't have the funds for that. Or most of the material ones actually."

"What is your budget?"

Daniel hesitated, considering what he should answer. Eventually, Daniel decided to trust the smiling Enchantress. "Fifty gold is my limit."

"That's sufficient," Kaylee said, smiling. "I'd even recommend you pick up two enchantments —if you have the slots—rather than one strong one. It'll give you more flexibility and be a better deal."

Daniel nodded, and Kaylee smiled, leading the man around the shop as she showed him the wares. Together, the pair narrowed down Daniel's choices until he had four items that he considered acceptable. The first was the most expensive—an amulet that would cost nearly forty-five gold alone.

Amulet of Lesser Perception
Effect: Enhances user aura to improve user's perception by +12%
Durability: 35/35
Item Class: Enchanted
Quality: Average

The amulet itself seemed to be less than useful on first glance. But Kaylee had explained that the increase in Perception would increase numerous skills like trap finding, tactics, combat sense and even his skill proficiency **Find Weakness**. When Kaylee let Daniel try the amulet on briefly, he felt his awareness expand. Even without activating the active portion of his Find Weakness proficiency,

Daniel felt his attraction to the weakness in Kaylee's structure—the way she jutted out one hip while standing, and the hollow in her throat, the moment when she exhaled. Daniel found himself unable to look away for some time, fascinated by the fall of her chest, and of the way a low breeze made her hair dance.

"Ahem."

"Sorry."

"It's okay. Increased Perception does that. It'll take you a few days to get used to the increase. But unlike many of your other choices, it's an enchantment that you can wear all the time."

"Right," Daniel said, taking the amulet off. It was too distracting to wear right now, especially while he was trying to make a smart decision. His next two choices were variations of the same type.

Lesser Ring of Flame

Effect: The Lesser Ring of Flame imbues the wearer's aura with a flame element. Deals 8 – 10 points of Fire Damage per successful attack.
Durability: 20/20
Item Class: Enchanted
Quality: Average

Lesser Ring of Cold
Effect: The Lesser Ring of Cold imbues the wearer's aura with the cold element. Deals 5-8 points of Cold Damage per successful attack. 10% chance of imbuing a slow effect on target. Slow effect is only partially cumulative.
Durability: 20/20
Item Class: Enchanted
Quality: Average

Both were direct damage attacks. In fact, the base damage increase from the ring of fire was as great as his hammer, though that did not take into account his strength and skill, of course. Still, the boost in damage was significant. On the other hand, the ring of cold provided less of a direct damage boost but did provide a secondary effect. And from Daniel's experience, the secondary effect could be quite useful.

"Of course, you understand that these attacks might have lower effects against certain monsters. For example, the ring of fire is not as effective in the first three levels of both—sorry, three—Dungeons. The demons have fire-imbued auras and so additional fire makes little difference to them," Kaylee warned.

"Of course." Daniel put the rings down and turned to the last item. This one was an earring. While Daniel knew that earrings were a common accessory among men and women, he had never seen himself as a person who wore an earring. But, the advantages were too great to pass up over a concern about fashion.

Lesser Earring of Revenge
Effect: The Lesser Earring of Revenge imbues the wearer's aura with a destructive effect against those with ill intent. Aura does 5-10 points of damage to attacker. Amount of damage varies depending on the amount of time attacker is in contact with aura and amount of damage dealt.
Durability: 17/17
Item Class: Enchanted
Quality: Average

The earring was an interesting enchanted piece. In particular, its effect directly attacked his opponent's aura, bypassing many common defenses like armor or a tough hide. That more than made up for the low amount of damage it did, especially since the attack would occur from his aura. So blocking an attack would as effectively damage a monster as getting hit—which was a big plus. It also meant that the earring was more effective against multiple attackers than the rings.

But, its low durability was a concern. While it was not likely to get damaged while it was under his helmet, Daniel still found himself slightly concerned. In addition, the earring itself was thirty-five gold, while each of the rings were only twenty-five. He could purchase both rings if he wished, but it would render them both ineffective—after all, cold and fire were directly in opposition.

Buying a ring and the earring on the other hand would wipe out his funds. And Daniel knew that he needed to upgrade his shield soon. Or at least replace it. Even if a simple shield was not that expensive, it was still an expense.

"Do you want to test them for compatibilities?" Kaylee asked, seeing Daniel hesitate. At Daniel's nod, the pair took the new twenty minutes putting on and testing the various accessories for any hidden incompatibilities. The issue with enchantments that affected the aura was that they could have unknown side-effects. Obviously, some—like fire and cold—were well known, but many more were just specific to an individual.

"Huh," Daniel said finally. As much as he liked the cold ring, it seemed that it had significant issues with his aura. Using it and any other enchanted item – other than his existing ring of experience – caused conflicts. Even the ring of experience was pushing it with the ring of cold. "I guess I'm not a cold person."

"It seems so," Kaylee said. She pushed the fire ring and earring forward. "This seemed to be a good combination for you. It is higher than your budget, but I doubt you'd find a more appropriate pair at your price range."

"Yeah…" Daniel scratched his head, lips pressed tight before he looked up at Kaylee. "Maybe there could be a discount?"

"Maybe…" Kaylee said, tapping the earring. "I could discount the entire pair by two gold. And that's because I made this."

"Two gold?" Daniel scratched his nose but then nodded firmly. "Okay. Done."

Kaylee smiled, and soon enough, Daniel had emptied his pouch of the pair. He quickly stored the ring away in his inventory, not wanting to accidentally set anyone on fire. As for the earring, Kaylee helped Daniel pierce his ear immediately. Unlike the other enchanted items, the earring was keyed towards intent—both Daniel's and his attackers. It was a more complicated piece of equipment, which was why it was also more expensive.

"It looks good," Kaylee said while Daniel pulled his hand down, forcing himself not to touch his ear. It was… well, strange. "Do come back if you ever need more work."

Daniel could only offer Kaylee a strained smile before he left. As he looked up and eyed the sun, Daniel realised it was later than he had expected. Speeding up his footsteps, the adventurer made his way to the Guild Hall to continue his training. No matter what, he could not slack off on his training, even with the new enchanted pieces.

Chapter 4

Two days later, the group reconvened before the entrance of Portos. The group was more somber this time as they fully understood the danger involved. The monsters within were tough, and more importantly, they were prone to delivering significant damage. A careless moment was all that was needed for one of their own to die. As such, this time, the group went through the pre-entrance procedures with uncharacteristic seriousness.

In a short time, the party soon found themselves facing a pair of Zarask once more. This time, the party was kitted out slightly differently and tested out some new tactics. Tula began the engagement by loosing a new arrow, one that flew straight at the Zarask's chest mouth. The creature clamped its lips shut automatically, but this only aided the workings of her arrow. On impact, the small crystal tip exploded and spread the liquid glue and spider silk extract, sealing the creature's mouth temporarily.

Behind Tula, Omrak heaved a throwing axe at the other monster even as he charged forwards. Rather than grabbing his sheathed sword, Omrak barrelled into the Zarask with his shoulder as the creature finished dodging his axe. Together, the pair fell to the dirt, the giant Northerner rolling away immediately even as the Zarask struggled to its feet. By this point, the rest of the team had caught up and peppered the prone monster with throwing knives and enchanted metal spikes while Tula held off the first monster with the edge of her bow.

Daniel moved forwards quickly, taking his place in the line and waiting until Tula fell back far enough. He timed his movement to gently bump against her back, warning her that he was there before the pair swiftly changed places, Daniel taking the Zarask's next blow with his shield. Together, the pair worked on containing the enraged monster whose initial enthusiasm waned as Daniel's new earring took its toll on the monster after each successful block.

Behind his helmet, Daniel found himself grinning. Even though the effect was significantly more muted through his shield, the creature's clawed hands were sizzling from contact with his aura. Already, he could tell the Zarask growing afraid of his shield, backing off as Daniel pushed ahead. A well-timed arrow took the Zarask in the shoulder, creating an opening that Daniel pursued aggressively. He stepped forward, shoulder braced behind his shield and thrust it forward, watching as the Zarask flinched away. As it turned its body to him, Daniel unleashed his **Double Strike**, crushing chest and arm in short order.

Once Daniel and Tula finished their opponent, they looked up to see Omrak's newly enchanted sword take the other Zarask's head right off.

"What was that?" Daniel asked. No one moved, their hearing blocked, and he groaned to himself, padding over and waving at Omrak to get his attention. He pointed to the sword and the blond Northerner grinned, holding it up for Daniel to look at.

The oversized sword had been cleaned and buffed; edges cleared in the time they had been gone. But, more interestingly, a series of runes had been etched down both sides of the sword. Daniel extended his hand towards the edge, feeling the way wind moved over the sword's edge, rippling. He tilted his head towards his friend, mouthing the word 'Wind'.

Omrak's happy nod was sufficient to confirm Daniel's assumption. It seemed that Omrak had his sword enchanted with a wind or air rune, giving the blade a new, sharper cutting edge. From the evidence, it seemed that the new enchantment was highly effective.

Tula tapped the others on the shoulder, gesturing for their attention, before pointing down the corridor. Daniel flushed slightly, nodding his acceptance as he pushed his curiosity aside. Later. He would check the new weapon later.

***

Four hours later, the group found themselves staring at a potentially fortuitous encounter. Facing them, in a large hall with multiple entrances and flanked by imposing statues of twelve-foot-tall Zarask, was a single large chest. The floor chest which contained the larger than normal Mana

Stone. Of course, along with the floor chest was the Floor Champion and its four compatriots that prowled the halls, snacking on the discarded remnants of an Adventurer's pack. The former owner was not to be seen.

Zarask Champion (Level 18)
HP: 270/270

As the group stared at their latest encounter, Daniel gestured the team to retreat. Quietly, they pulled away from the monsters until they were a safe distance back and out of hearing range. Crouched down together, Daniel risked pulling out the earplug from one ear, gesturing for the team to follow suit.

"Do we want to do this?" Daniel asked, looking at the group. Their last four hours had gone well. Between the new equipment and tactics, the team had managed to achieve a decent record this time around with few injuries. Daniel had barely had to use his Mana thus far, leaving him nearly filled and ready to heal. Still, a Champion was always much tougher. Just by the ten-foot-tall size, it was clear this was not going to be a simple fight.

"You want to leave a Champion and floor stone behind?" Rob said incredulously.

"That's a yes from Rob then," Daniel said.

"No," Tula said.

"I would not shame my family by turning down such honorable battle," Omrak rumbled.

Asin hesitated for a second, then looked between the group. She looked particularly hard at Tula, who declined to explain her vote. In one of her hands, a throwing knife flipped round and round from finger to finger, spinning around her hand in nervous habit.

"Daniel?" Asin yowled.

"One Champion. Four Zarask," Daniel thought aloud. "I can handle the Champion alone I think. At least, for a bit. That leaves the other four. Asin and Omrak can probably handle one of the Zarask each and take them down. But that leaves the other two."

"I can delay another," Rob said. "I have created and recharged a number of my ice and water traps. They will slow down my target, especially if I focus only on them."

"Tula?" Daniel turned towards the range.

"No," Tula said, shaking her head. "Not good odds."

"Bah," Rob said and crossed his arms. As Daniel opened his mouth to cast his vote, Rob added. "If I split my enchantments, I can slow both. But for a much shorter time. Asin or Omrak must finish their target faster."

"Mine," Asin said. She then pointed at Tula. "Help."

"Together?" Daniel muttered, considering. Omrak was fast with his new weapon too, which was the reason for the split. While Omrak could handle the Champion, it was better for him to be fighting the other four and potentially picking up those that escaped Rob's traps. Adding his weapon to the fight would mean that the minions would be dealt with faster too.

"Three."

"Huh?" Daniel said, looking at Asin confused.

"The Catkin means that there are three votes now to go in. Your vote is unimportant," Rob said.

Daniel found himself frowning at the Enchanter's words and turned to Tula, searching her face for her feelings on this. The Ranger just shrugged her shoulders, readjusting the lie of her cloak.

"I guess we're going in," Daniel said. Once he confirmed everyone knew their roles, the Healer gestured for everyone to replace their earplugs. Tightening his grip on his hammer, Daniel waved everyone forwards.

***

As the party entered the hall again, traversing deeper, they split their usual line formation into a wider one. Behind them, a set of simple tripwire traps and flares were set-up to alert them of reinforcements from behind. This fight was one that required all of them after all.

The Zarask noticed the party as the group spread out, letting out growls and yips that were unheard by the Adventurers. The Champion stood up, hands falling open as its chest mouth opened to release a scream. An arrow winged forwards, blocked by one of its minions which batted the arrow out of the air. For its trouble, its arm was smeared by the sticky mixture, gluing its fingers together.

Uninterrupted, the Champion howled, the noise joined soon after by the other Zarask. The combined sonic assault staggered the party of Adventurers, cutting through their hearing protection and making their very bones tremble and organs hurt. Daniel coughed, feeling blood fill his mouth as he bit his own tongue to regain his balance and shake off the effects.

Looking around, he noticed his friends staggering under the assault. Making up his mind, Daniel quickly began casting Healer's Mark. Slapping Rob on the shoulder, he layered the healing spell on the Enchanter, helping the Selkie stand straight as the volume dissipated.

Omrak, enraged, charged forwards, breaking the line of their careful group. Behind him, Asin took off while Tula continued to flank the group, her bow singing as more arrows flew forwards. This time, she targeted the minions, managing to web two mouths shut before Omrak clashed with the group. Wind-enchanted sword in hand, the Northerner took large, curving swings to ward off his attackers.

The Champion, forced behind his minions as protection earlier, stomped around the group. With Rob receiving healing, Daniel took off at a dead run in an attempt to head off the Champion before he joined the fight against Omrak and the now-arrived Catkin.

As the Champion finally managed to make its way around the group, Daniel arrived as well and threw himself into an impromptu shoulder-charge and **Shield Bash**. Triggering the Skill as he flew through the air, his arm shot forwards to slam into the Champion, staggering the monster. Having attracted its attention, Daniel was struck and sent staggering to the side as he landed.

Tiny balls rolled across the ground, releasing streams of water. These streams reached and grasped, forming into tendrils that gripped and grabbed at legs. The Zarask paused as they swarmed the pair of fighters in their encirclement, letting up for a brief moment their assault as they attempted to extract themselves. A few seconds later, even more enchanted weapons landed, shattering and releasing a cloud of freezing Mana-laden gas. On contact with the water, the formerly easily broken tendrils of water froze, attaching themselves to skin. For a brief moment, the Zarask were caught, unable to move, and Tula took full advantage. A **Storm of Arrows** landed among the group, each arrow an empowered version filled with a strength-sapping poison. As the Zarask pulled themselves free, feathered and injured, they tore skin and left weeping wounds of frostbitten flesh behind.

In the meantime, Daniel found his footing and lashed out at the Champion with **Perrin's Blow**. The empowered strike, targeted at the lower floating rib that Daniel sensed to be a weakness in the Champion, threw the monster away from the main scramble. Having drawn the Champion's full attention, Daniel hunkered down under his wooden shield and plate armor, focusing on deflecting earth-shaking blows with his shield and weapon at an angle. Even then, Daniel quickly found his arms numbing under the repeated assault. If he could, he would have called for help, but none could hear him.

Time slowed down, each clawed strike another saved second, another moment that his friends could make use of to win their fight. His **Find Weakness** skill kept informing Daniel of potential areas to strike against the Champion, but Daniel could not afford to take the chance. Even potential openings were discarded in the brutal calculus of stamina and speed that Daniel had to make, refusing to trade a chance blow for wasted strength.

Another blow, this one caught slightly too slowly, sent his hammer skipping out of his hand. The loop around his wrist pulled his entire arm out of place, a mistake that opened his chest to a brutal kick. It threw Daniel backwards even as the Champion's foot was left smoking. On his buttocks, Daniel scrambled to rise as the Champion threw its head back and howled.

Once more, Daniel found the sonic attack resounding within his bones. Closer now, the attack was even more brutal. But instead of a general area attack, the Champion looked towards Daniel and cupped its hands together, focusing the howling attack. It struck Daniel directly, wracking the Healer with pain.

As suddenly as the scream started, it shut up. Blearily, his vision tinged in red, Daniel saw a throwing knife stuck in the monster's throat. As the Champion staggered backwards, attempting to claw the sparking knife out of its mouth, an arrow joined it. Then another.

A wracking cough forced Daniel to roll to the side, spitting blood out of his mouth as he attempted to clear his throat. He scrambled at his helmet clasp, finally freeing his face as he gulped down desperately needed air, forgetting for a moment about the fight around him. As his breath came to him, Daniel reached for his Mana, casting a simple **Minor Healing II** on himself first before layering a **Healer's Mark**. As he staggered to his feet, he turned back to the battle only to see it finished.

Around him, there were only the Mana crystals of the slain Zarask and the fallen body of the Champion. Standing over the corpse, a no longer glowing Omrak stood, his sword plunged directly into the monster's chest where its heart would be.

"Oh. I guess I could have waited," Daniel said.

He frowned, touching his ear, and realised he could not even hear himself. With a sigh, he slumped to the ground and just lay on the cold floor, enjoying the cool comfort. Later, he'd heal everyone else. But for now, he was the most injured of the group and, on Healer's orders, he was going to have a lie-down.

Chapter 5

Cleaning up after the Dungeon run was simple enough. By the time Daniel had finished healing himself and the rest of the team, no one wanted to continue, so they had carefully explored and found the way down to the next floor. Using the staircase, they then transferred themselves to the exit. Tula was grateful enough that both Asin and Rob were willing to deal with the disposition of their loot. Running a Dungeon was always more stressful than a day's journey in the outlands. It was, Tula believed, because in a Dungeon you knew you were going to be battling monsters at some point. In the outlands, you could go days without a violent encounter.

Tula sighed, shaking her head. Whether it was stressful or not, she would soon be leaving Silverstone and its Dungeons. The expedition to the west of Brad was not breaking new ground, but any expedition that passed near the untamed lands like the expedition planned to needed a Ranger. Even if she did not want to go, her orders from the Western Ivy were clear.

And, in truth, it would be good to get out of the city and see her family. Just because she enjoyed talking did not mean she liked crowds. And the city was nothing if not filled with people. All of them talking too loud, crowding too close, and refusing to bathe often enough.

Tula ran a hand through her hair again, picking up the small brush she had been gifted, she brushed her short hair again. Hot baths were a luxury that she would miss. As she stared at the scarred visage in the mirror, she found her lips twitching up slightly. Baths and those silly party members of hers. Still, the time together with them had been helpful. She was now two-thirds of the way to Level 16 after all the adventuring they had done.

"Best get moving," Tula said, shaking her head. "If I don't, Asin is just going to have Erin give us too heavily spiced meats."

Putting her brush away, Tula turned and looked around her room. The bed was made, and her belongings were all stored in her pouch. She could leave right now and never come back and not be missing a single thing. As Tula reached for and picked up her bow, she nodded. Good.

A short journey took Tula from her inn to Erin's where the group had decided to meet. The food was good, plentiful, and Erin was known to keep trouble out. It made the inn very popular among Adventurers, especially after a day's delving.

"Over here!" Omrak roared when he spotted Tula standing just inside the door, looking through the inn for them. She trotted over while Omrak relieved another table of a stool, dropping it down with a thump. "You took a while, friend Tula. Everyone else is here!"

"I wanted a bath," Tula said and sniffed in Omrak's direction. "You, obviously, made a different choice."

"I bathed two days ago," Omrak said. "And I wiped myself down with oil just last night."

"That is not helping your case," Daniel said.

Beside Daniel and opposite Omrak, Asin leaned over to prod Rob in the side. When he howled and sat-up, she flashed him a toothy grin and then prodded him again.

"What? Speak, you confounded feline!" Rob snapped.

"Change." Poke.

"Change what?" Rob said.

"Tula."

"Fine," Rob said as he batted away her clawed finger. Muttering unkind words about sharp nails, Rob changed places with Tula.

"Thank you," Tula said to Asin as she took her seat. "Did you all order already?"

"Just the first couple of plates," Daniel said. "But we have some non-spicy meats coming."

"Good," Tula said. She snagged a skewer of vegetables, biting into the cooked onion and pepper meal.

"Share." A small pouch dropped beside Tula who juggled the skewer, her pouch, and the contents of the smaller pouch before sliding it all away.

"Not going to count it?" Rob said, his brows drawn down with disapproval.

"I trust you."

"Trust is good. But you should still verify," Rob said.

"My choice," Tula said. "As we've discussed."

"It would make me feel better if you checked it. As I've said before."

"Tough," Tula said, sticking her tongue out before she took another bite of her skewer. She then snagged three more skewers as one of Erin's waitress dropped a new plate of skewered meat onto the table. This one did not have the telltale red glow of the other skewers.

The group fell to drinking and eating, and their discussion turning to the fights earlier in the day. It was a time-honored tradition, a debriefing and discussion of the fear, the terror that they had all faced. A sharing of experiences that helped their minds and souls to come to terms with what had happened. It was a good ritual, one that Tula knew was conducted by the Rangers too. Which, considering how taciturn so many of their members were, said much of the effectiveness of the talks. In the end, the group finished debriefing, their minds and emotions settled like the food in their stomachs.

"What are you planning tomorrow?" Tula said curiously. Tomorrow, she would be leaving. Still, she was curious what the team planned. Back to Artos? Or would they retry Portos to gain familiarity?

"Tomorrow?" Omrak looked confused as he spoke. "We go with you, do we not?"

"What? No. That's my expedition," Tula said, frowning. Omrak might be a little naïve at times, but he was not stupid. Though he did have a tendency to not listen when they spoke.

"Yes," Asin said.

"That's right." Both Omrak and Tula agreed with Asin's word. When Tula saw Asin grinning at the confusion she caused when both Adventurers realised that her ambiguous answer could be applied to them both, Tula reached over and smacked the playful Catkin.

"That isn't helping."

"Yes."

"Enough, Asin. Stop teasing them," Daniel said. "Omrak is right. We are coming with you."

"What!" Tula yelped.

"Well, we took a team vote and decided we were getting tired of Dungeons. And an expedition led by a real Ranger sounded like a great experience," Daniel said. "So, we joined the expedition."

"You can't do that!" Tula said.

"Is friend Tula angry with us?" Omrak leaned over and whispered in his usual loud manner to Rob. "Were we not meant to join friend Tula?"

"I think she's just a little surprised," Rob said. "Right, Tula?"

"Sorry. Sorry. You're right. I'm not saying you can't come. I just didn't expect you to come. You know? This wasn't the plan."

"But you are happy for us to come, are you not?" Daniel said, leaning across from Asin.

Tula fell silent as she met Daniel's intense gaze. She paused, forced to consider how she felt about the announcement. Did she want her team—her ex or previously ex team—to come? After a moment's consideration, Tula realised that she was happy to have them. A team that she knew, that she trusted on her back? That was something most Rangers longed for. Too often they ended up guiding strangers, which led to conflict and increased danger. It was just that the expedition was going to be going home. For her friends to see that, for…

"No. It's fine," Tula said, offering Daniel a half-smile. It would be fine. They were her friends after all.

"Good. Because we can't back out now anyway," Rob said. "The damage to our party standing would be enormous."

Tula snorted while Asin just let out a little snort of laughter.

"Right, now that you know our secret. Let's talk gear," Daniel said, turning serious. "Here's what we have purchased. If we need something else, we have a few hours in the morning to pick it up. But, I think we're good."

Tula leaned forwards to listen in, head cocked to the side as the healer began listing their preparations, all the while squashing the squirming mass of concern in her stomach. It would be fine.

***

"Kind of reminds you of our first guard request, doesn't it?" Daniel said to Asin the next morning. Gathered in a small square just off the main boulevard, the Adventuring team watched as the expedition got itself together. Multiple carriages were pulled over to the side where the caravan master's secretary was reviewing the wear of the carriages and beast of burden, ensuring that they were all up to the expedition's standards. At the same time, the caravan master was interrogating the carriage drivers—the Drovers and Wagon Masters being forced to provide details of their Skills. For the most part, it would not be important, but a good caravan master would still ensure he knew the full extent of his people's Skills.

"Team leader," Asin said, jerking her head to where an adventuring team walked in.

Daniel turned to stare at the group, the only other Adventuring team on this expedition. As Daniel watched the group walk forwards, he reviewed what he knew about the team. A yellow tier Advanced Adventuring team, they outranked their own team by seniority, leaving their team leader in charge. The team itself was one of the Seven Stone's many sponsored teams, and Daniel could not help but admire their equipment. All seven of the adventuring team wore a light dark-grey cloak whose inside lining held the tailored enchantment runes that kept their wearers warm, dry and cool. The 'Adventurers Cloaks' were much in demand and cost at least thirty gold each.

"Daniel Chai? Of the DAO?" the group leader asked as he approached. The tall blond man wore the grey cloak over his shiny plate armor with casual ease. To Daniel's surprise, the man made no sound when he moved, nor did he seem encumbered by the steel plate mail at all. Daniel, on the other hand, was dressed only in his iron breastplate, eschewing the majority of his armor for comfort.

"That would be me," Daniel said. "You're Craig Morris of the Seven Stones."

"That would be me. You did your homework," Craig said. "This is Vivian, Bjarne, Uppulu, Hjalmar, Elisa, and Sumuhan."

Daniel's gaze flicked over the party, who acknowledged the pair each time Craig spoke. One of the first things Daniel noticed was the way that a couple of members of the party moved, favoring old—or perhaps fresh—injuries. Wrapped bandages, a hitch in a step. It spoke to the healer within Daniel, but the healer made no offer to relieve their pain. He had no desire to be mobbed by cheapskate Adventurers again.

Vivian was dressed in light, untreated green leather, the scales of the monster that it came from still attached. From his recollection, she was a sorcerer instead of a mage—untrained in the channelling of magic via a formal school with her spells all coming from her Skills. It meant that she was much less versatile than a real mage, but she had the advantage of being a faster caster since she only had to invoke her Skills. It was, in some ways, similar to Daniel's own use of Minor Healing. Well, before he had progressed it by study.

Bjarne was bigger, taller, and dressed in a chainmail hauberk with leather and cloth padding otherwise. Daniel noted that the cloth padding he wore underneath the light leather on his arms glowed slightly, golden stitching through the cloth indicating it was likely to be enchanted. Bjarne had a short sword sheathed on his waist, but he carried a halberd behind his shield.

Uppulu was armed and armored very similar to Bjarne, except that the dark-skinned warrior wielded a leaf-bladed spear rather than a halberd. Otherwise, the pair seemed to favour lighter armor and a larger shield than Craig. Of note to Daniel was Uppulu's footwear which consisted of lace-up sandals with tiny wings on the end.

Hjalmar was a change from the previous warriors, being thinner, shorter, and overall smaller. Clad in light leather armor, the archer carried a simple recurve bow that he held unstrung in one hand. Even standing still, Hjalmar kept cracking his neck, shrugging his shoulders and otherwise stretching out.

Elisa was the Seven Stones team's other long-range fighter, the young woman wielding a recurve bow as well. Daniel could tell that her weapon was enchanted, the gilding along the edge of the bow a clear indication. When Daniel looked over to her, she flashed the young healer a bright smile, causing Uppulu to frown.

Sumuhan was the last of the team to be introduced, and he was also the only Beastkin. Sumuhan was a rarer Beastkin, a goat-variant, unlike the majority predator Beastkin. Sumuhan's snout was longer than Asin's, with a long, white wispy beard trailing from his face and well-polished horns on his top. The Goatkin towered over the group, standing around six feet eight inches, and on his back, he carried three javelins. As for his main weapon, the Goatkin held a simple maul.

"Your team look very competent," Daniel said, after letting his gaze pass over the group one last time.

"As does yours," Craig said as he nodded over Daniel's shoulder. Daniel turned, smiling slightly when he realised that his team were entering at last, Omrak in the lead. In short order, the groups introduced themselves to one another.

"As the senior team, we will be taking charge and assigning roles," Craig said. "Is that an issue?"

"Not at all," Daniel said.

"Except when I say otherwise," Tula said, the Ranger stepping forward to join the conversation.

"If it involves exploring new paths, stop timing, and dealing with new monsters, I do have final authority."

"We're on a charted road," Hjalmar said as he crossed his arms. "Your Ranger garbage is not needed."

"Charted road or not, it's still considered the outlands," Tula said. "If it was not, I would not be required to join you. As per Guild covenant 1.9.3 on expeditions, a Ranger's authority is paramount in all expeditions."

"There we go again. The Ranger is throwing around her weight," Hjalmar said, rolling his eyes. "Just because they've got a 'better' Class. I bet she's not even Level 20 yet, and she thinks she can order us around."

"Hjalmar…" Craig said.

"No. This is the kind of bureaucratic garbage that gets Adventurers killed," Hjalmar said.

"It's Adventurers like you who refuse to follow Ranger orders that get people killed on expeditions," Tula said, stepping forwards as she glowered at the man.

"Look, can we talk about this?" Daniel said, trying to find some peace.

"Do not worry, Adventurer Chai. There will be no problems here," the caravan master said as he walked over, having seen the brewing problem. "Team leader Craig. Handle your man. The Guild rules are clear as are my expedition rules. The

Ranger is in charge when there is a clear and obvious threat from outland monsters.

"Are we clear?"

Craig flushed and nodded. When Hjalmar tried to speak again, Craig went as far as to growl at his friend.

"Good. Ranger Tula, thank you for joining the expedition," the caravan master said.

"My pleasure," Tula said.

"If you are ready, the caravan will depart now."

"Go ahead. For the first ten miles, there is little of concern," Tula said, her face impassive. "I will lead the way nonetheless."

"Of course." Once again the caravan master nodded to Tula before leaving, soon followed by Craig after he distributed the group. The sullen Hjalmar was left to stand guard at the back, alone.

As the caravan trundled out of town, Rob who had been assigned to stand with Daniel leaned over and whispered, "That was an auspicious start."

All Daniel could do was smile wryly in response.

Chapter 6

A gentle breeze blew, pushing against Asin's whiskers and ruffling her fur. She trotted beside the carriage, happy to be out of the city. As much as the Catkin had grown up in the city, her expanded senses meant that she would always find the stench of urban life just a little much. Not that the outdoors did not have their fair share of offensive odours, but they were often less concentrated. As Asin drew a deep breath, she tasted the scents of the road—dust, gravel and horse droppings mixed with the grass, leaves and rotting vegetation of the meadows beside. There was a slight smell of fungi coming from the wind along with rotten wood, but it was the smell of fresh rabbit that made her mouth water. Too bad it was off in the forest itself, hiding out of sight of the caravan train. And, next to her, the smell of goat and human, the Beastkin having a distinctive scent compared to real animals.

"Surprised to see your group here," Sumuhan said, breaking the silence as he scratched at one bandaged arm. Now that they were out of the city, speech was much simpler and easier.

"Why?" Asin said.

"You have a healer. If we had one, we'd be in the Dungeon every day," Sumuhan said. The goat's voice was rougher and higher than a normal human's voice with a tendency to wobble as he spoke, similar to an actual animal.

Asin could only shrug, her tail waving at Sumuhan's statement. What Sumuhan mentioned was very similar to their normal method of raiding.

It was the biggest difference between their team and many others. A normal Adventuring team had to be extremely careful about injuries, forcing them to take each level with caution. Most parties entered the Dungeon injured, Adventurers favoring torn muscles or tendons, aches and bruises from previous encounters, and the occasional broken bone. Minor injuries that hampered but not did not stop the Adventurers from delving.

But a single major injury—a broken bone, a stab, or a cut that opened up torsos or wounds—could stop a party's progress. Worse, as Asin knew, injuries had a tendency to snowball in a fight. A mistake and one Adventurer would go down. In an Advanced Dungeon that often meant the outnumbered Adventurers would be forced to fight even more monsters alone. That would result in more risks, more injuries. A single mistake and two to three members could find themselves injured.

At which point, an Adventuring party would have to decide to go ahead injured, use up precious and expensive healing potions, or pull out and rest. Many a party, like Sumuhan's, would do the wise thing and rest. It was better when there were multiple injured parties in some ways, for it allowed the entire group to rest, heal, and then enter whole. In some cases, when the injuries were half-healed, groups would take up quests, earning them coin while not placing them in as much danger.

Like expeditions.

Expeditions themselves were often priced to attract Adventuring parties at a higher payout than normal. The long, boring journeys often required the groups to leave their home base, reducing the amount of time a group could Level. Unlike guard quests which travelled between populous locations, expeditions went from populous to the outlands, forcing the group to stay with the expedition the entire time. The length of the trips and the variable danger of expeditions meant that they had to pay better than normal quests.

But only in relation to normal quests for an 'average' Dungeon delving team. For groups like Asin's, who could heal and be back in the Dungeon every other day or so, their earning levels were much lower. In fact, Asin hummed to herself, she had been hesitant about this trip herself. Giving up all that coin… It had not sat well with her. Hesitant or not, since the rest of the group had been excited with the idea when Rob had brought it up, she had gone along with it.

"So why did you come?" Sumuhan said, having given up waiting for her to answer without prompting.

"Experience," Asin said. "Expedition. Ranger."

"All expeditions have Rangers."

"Not all," Asin said. "Availability."

"True. We are lucky…" Sumuhan said. "*We can speak in Beastkin if you wish.*"

"*Yes, easier to speak,*" Asin said. She turned towards the back, spotting a lone trudging figure. "*Not all your friends are happy.*"

"*Hjalmar? He is never happy. Not since we voted Craig in as the new party leader,*" Sumuhan said.

"*Why?*"

"*Party issues.*" Sumuhan turned his head away from Asin, staring at the clump of forest they were approaching before deciding that there were no threats there. Not that any threats this close to the city was likely. Not with the amount of traffic on the road. Traffic was slow enough on the busy roadway that many members of the caravan were walking to ease their backs. Springed steel shocks or not, it was not comfortable sitting on the wagons for any length of time. "*They treat you well, young one?*"

"*You're not that old,*" Asin said. Though, she had to admit, Sumuhan was aged for an Advanced Adventurer being in his late twenties. For a Goatkin who rarely lived older than fifty, he was more than half done. And adventuring was young man's game for the most part. "*But they are good. Many of us have been together for over a year. Tula and Rob are newer, but they treat me fair.*"

"*Good.*" Unspoken lay the fact that being more bestial than many of their kin, they faced even more prejudice. There were guilds and

86

Adventuring groups that refused to take Beastkin that looked as bestial as they did as concerns over their 'animal nature' failing in the Dungeon was still prevalent. Even if it was quite untrue.

Talk after that turned to the usual discussion between Adventurers—of weapons and spells, tactics and monsters. The shop talk of people who find themselves dealing in violence on a regular basis. Even if, unlike what the general public might envision, it was a little less common.

***

Four days later, Daniel yawned as he sat on the lead carriage, watching the surroundings trundle by. Once they left the main roadways that linked up the major cities of Brad, the group had swung north and west, heading for the outlands and the final destination of the expedition. Once they reached their destination in another two weeks, the plan was to spend a month in the outlands, hunting, gathering and otherwise collecting the bounty of the wilderness. Over the course of the expedition, the expedition master would sell or barter the numerous essential items to the Hunters, Trappers, Outlanders, and the villagers for the goods they had collected. In time, the continual immigration of commoners and the civilizing influence of more people would see the development of larger villages and the birth of new towns.

That is, if the Orcs that lived further south of the northwestern forests did not send a War Party to deal with the encroaching villagers. As a landlocked nation, Brad could not expand farther east as it came up against the larger Empire of Kobyzcha. To the southeast, the Beastkin nation of Garhwa bordered the Empire—a semi-vassal state that existed on a populous and varied land. To the south, Brad had expanded as far as it could before it abutted the no-man's land of the Esenbey Desert. The nomadic tribes that lived there claimed the desert as much as any could call it theirs. While the desert tribes did raid the villages once in a while, it was overall a peaceful relationship. And, of course, to the southwest and west, the sprawling Orc nations. If Brad had any reason for surviving against the greater Empire of Kobyzcha, it was because the Empire enjoyed the safeguard of Brad. Not that it stopped the Empire from building its famous fortress cities along the border between the two.

"Why the smile, young man?" the driver who had introduced himself as Grey said when he spotted Daniel smiling wryly to himself.

"History. We used to dominate this continent. Even have it named after ourselves. And now, we're well." Daniel shrugged.

"We're still here, aren't we?" Grey said and then leaned over to spit a stream of betel juice to the side. "Lots of nations can't say that. Even the ones that took our lands later."

"True. Two millennia is a long time," Daniel said. Brad's days of glory were long in the past. The once-mighty empire had been brought low by internal politics, and two Master Class and four Advanced Class Dungeon breaks in the midst of a three-hundred-year-long civil war. Add in the on-going battles with the invading Orcs from overseas during the periods of peace in the civil war, and the empire had shrunk and shrunk again. Each had drained the strength of the once-mighty empire, slowly forcing it to draw its effective area of control. In that gap, monsters and other nations had claimed the land.

In truth, few Adventurers knew much about the history of Brad. Daniel himself would have been mostly ignorant too, if not for bedtime talks with Khy'ra. It was, in her view, for the best. Too much concern about the former glories of the past would lead to another wasteful war of conquest. Those wars, in Khy'ra's view, were one of the main reasons that the empire had fallen – the diversion of Adventurers from the important task of clearing Dungeons.

"Two? You mean three, no?" Grey said.

Daniel shook his head. "Two."

"Nah, that ain't right. My ma always said it was three," Grey reiterated. "You should take it from me. She was capital educated."

Daniel opened his mouth to correct the man again and then stared at Grey's mulish face. After a moment, he decided not to push the matter. After all, his information was second-hand too. Even if it was from an old Elf. "Did you ever go? To the capital?"

"Nah. Silverstone is good enough for me," Grey said. "Big enough to get lost in, not so big you got too many of the wrong kind around."

Daniel stiffened but kept his voice neutral as he said. "Wrong kind?"

"Nobles."

"Oh," Daniel relaxed, refusing the offer of mint-wrapped betel nuts as Grey spat out his old set and added a new wad. "Not really met any."

Ahead of them, Tula had paused, waving to the group to slow down. A hand dropped, and Daniel retrieved his crossbow, working the cocking mechanism.

"Trouble?" Grey asked, the driver tapping his chest where a gold amulet sat.

"Yes." Daniel's eyes narrowed.

Well. It was a little too much to ask for the entire expedition to be quiet.

***

"What do we have, Ranger Tula?" Sava the caravan master asked Tula when the group reached the crouching Ranger. She walked over at an angle, her body turned towards the right of the road.

90

"Spligo," Tula said, turning away to face the direction of the threat fully now as she spoke. The arrow she held loosely to her bow continued to point in the direction of the rise that hid the monsters.

Sava hissed while Daniel made a face, pulling out another pair of crossbow bolts from his quiver as well as his hammer. He briefly debated his shield and then discarded the idea, preferring to keep his hand free for gripping hold of the wagon.

"How many?" Sava asked.

"A full pack," Tula said. "Nine adults. Six children. They took down a Bone Bison just over the ridge."

"Good," Sava said. "Recommendations?"

"Go slow. Be ready to run," Tula said. "If they are eating, they should be satisfied. Archers will fire when I do. We will attack only if we are attacked."

"Spligo are pests," Craig said, having joined the lead wagon on foot. "There are only fifteen of them. We can take them."

"Not our job," Tula said, shaking her head. Sava looked relieved when Tula spoke. "We'll send a missive when we are clear."

"The bounty on Spligo is five silver each. And their teeth and glands are quite prized," Craig said. "Left alone, such a large pack will split when the pups are grown."

"Not our job." Tula turned around to stare at Craig, her voice growing firmer. "We get the caravan master to his location and back. Safely."

Craig's lips tightened, but he nodded shortly. Sava smiled when he saw Craig walk off, inclining his head towards Tula. "Thank you, Ranger. This is why expedition master's like myself prefer having Rangers in-charge. Adventurers are a little… enthusiastic." Daniel stirred in his seat, and Sava flashed a quick smile at the young man. "No offence meant."

"None taken," Daniel said. He could understand Craig's desire. Five silver was a decent amount for a monster.

In short order, the entire caravan had been informed. Outside of a token force on the left, the regular guards and Adventurers shifted their attention to the right. Grey clicked his tongue and flicked the reins, getting his horses moving forwards at a slow trot. Once over the hills, Daniel caught sight of the Spligo.

The Spligo existed in that nebulous void of pest and threat. An individual Spligo was not dangerous. A pack of Spligo, on the other hand, were dangerous enough to take down a Bone Bison. Worse, in a single season, the Spligo might birth three or four times.

As for the Spligo itself, the monster looked like a thinner, flatter wolf with an oval face. Instead of a single set of jaws, the Spligo's mouth parted like a flower, razor-sharp teeth lining the snout where a mobile tongue-tentacle writhed, its barbed appendage used to wrap and drag bodies and limbs toward it. From what Daniel recalled, the monster's saliva was a mild paralytic, while its claws were surprisingly blunt.

"Let's just take this slow," Daniel whispered as he pointed the crossbow in the direction of the monsters. The group was hunched over the corpse of the Bone Bison, their long tongues wrapping around dead flesh to rip and pull into their maws. It was a sickening sight, especially when the monsters dipped their tongues into the monster's torso, moving within to rip and eat the viscera.

"Slow. I got slow." Grey fingered the solid steel crowbar that lay between the two of them. "Just hope they're happy with their meal.

"Yes. Slow. Can't outrun them, so we go slow," Daniel muttered. Beside the pair, Tula walked with a pair of arrows held in one hand and another arrow already nocked. She looked back and glared at the talking pair, making Daniel duck his head in embarrassment. After all this time, he knew that the Ranger disliked noise— calling it an unnecessary additional factor.

When the caravan was directly opposite the pack, Tula stopped walking and took a large step away from the road. She then just stood there, bow held low and ready while she stared at the monsters. The Spligo, having caught sight of the group, were all on their feet, dark eyes following the movements of the caravan before locking onto the still, tiny Ranger. An errant wind caught the edges of her brown hair, held down by a brimmed green and brown hat, playing with it and the edges of her clothing. It was the only thing that seemed to move as the Ranger stared down the monsters.

As the wagon trundled past the group, Daniel turned in his seat, his gaze drawn towards the largest member of the pack. The Spligo had been feasting at the shattered chest of the bison but now focused its attention on the group. A stretched head saw the creature's maw open up, showing the rows of sharp teeth on each portion of the monster's snout. From the second wagon where Hjalmar sat, the driver let out an involuntary yelp. As one, the monsters turned their heads to fix on the driver.

"Ba'al," Hjalmar swore, raising his bow and drawing the arrow back. A hand rested on his cheek as he exhaled. The Adventurer was one of many who tensed and readied themselves for the impending charge.

"Hold!" Tula's whispered words froze the group. The Ranger was one of the few who had not raised her bow. In fact, the Ranger took a step forwards, meeting the gaze of the pack fearlessly as they refocused on the Ranger.

As Daniel's wagon rolled up the next hill, fast taking him outside of view of the group, the Adventurer reluctantly turned away from the confrontation behind him. As the new lead, Daniel knew that it was up to him to ensure they did not just run into another group of monsters. Teeth clenched, Daniel scanned the area in front of him, searching for problems.

It was an agonizing wait as the caravan made its way past the Spligo. Caravan after caravan, they crested the hill before passing out of sight of the monsters. Impatient, Daniel would look behind at times, counting the number of caravans, straining his ears for the signs of battle.

Minutes turned into an hour, Daniel relaxing when he realised that there was no sign of pursuit. But the Healer could not relax entirely as Tula did not return to take her spot scouting ahead. In time, Sava rode forwards, gesturing for Grey to find a clearing. In the clearing, the caravan drivers took the short rest to water and groom their horses, checking on their loads and ensuring nothing had shifted.

"Sava?" Daniel called out to caravan master when he still could not see Tula.

"Yes, Adventurer Chai?" Sava said, turning away from handling a problem with a carriage driver.

"Tula?"

"The Ranger is behind us. She wanted to ensure the Spligo were truly letting us go," Sava said.

"We're waiting for her?" Daniel said.

"Of course," Sava said.

Relieved, Daniel took to the road while Craig ordered the remainder of the group around. In about fifteen minutes, a short camouflage-wearing figure appeared, loping at a ground-eating pace towards the group. Daniel exhaled, feeling the tension in his body disappearing as his teammate arrived.

That went as well as could be expected. If not better. Maybe having a Ranger on-hand really did make a difference.

Chapter 7

"UP! Up, you damn Adventurers. To arms!"

The roar shot Daniel out of his bedroll, his hand immediately closing on his enchanted hammer. Daniel rolled to his feet, his other hand scrambling for the straps of his shield even as he blinked the sleep from his eyes. He had just fallen asleep, his turn on night watch done. Or, it had at least felt just a few minutes ago, though from the way the logs in the fire had burnt down, it might had been a little longer.

"Where?" Daniel called, head turning as he searched for the monsters.

"South," Uppulu said. The spear wielder slapped a brooch pinned to his side, and Daniel watched as a light glow of blue surrounded the man. He took off after his actions, heading for the grunts and growls that Daniel now recognised were coming from that direction.

Up on his feet, Daniel started moving forwards and found Rob and Asin joining him. A few seconds later, Craig joined up with the majority of his people. A pair of arrows flew above their heads, disappearing into the darkness.

"Vivian, light!" Craig called out orders. "Daniel, form your team up and take the left. We'll take the right."

A flare of light illuminated their surroundings, allowing Daniel to see the carnage ahead of him. A pair of the caravan guards were standing beside Omrak and Uppulu, holding off their attackers—a pack of Spligo. Even as the light illuminated the air, Daniel could see how Omrak bled from his sides as he twisted to dodge a grasping tongue and sliced at another. The floppy, slimy mass bled from numerous cuts, but even a full-strength blow by the Northerner did not manage to sever the ropy mass of elastic muscle.

Another arrow flashed and caught one of the Spligo in the side of its mouth, pinning the folded back portion of its snout to its body. It howled, shaking its head and tongue, causing the writhing tentacle to miss. But the damage was not lethal, and the Spligo took advantage of the newly illuminated surroundings to spread out, away from the defenders.

"Omrak's poisoned," Daniel said in realisation. In fact, as he watched how a guard stumbled as he was dragged forwards and out of the impromptu shield wall, the entire group of defenders were. "Asin. You're in charge. I need to heal them!"

"Yes." The pair darted further to the left, Asin pulling a knife from her shoulder holster and tossing it at the first Spligo to make itself a target. The knife exploded into numerous copies as Asin triggered **Fan of Knives**, the glinting, sparking knives stunning the creature as the electric damage from her aura passed through it as her knives landed. A second later, a pair of enchanted spikes rammed into the creature from the sky, dropping the Spligo to its knees.

"**Minor Healing**," Daniel intoned as he raced towards the guards. The first wash of power, formed from the spell formula within his mind, shot out from his hand and hit the most severely injured of the guards. The healing was unfortunately timed however, the sudden burst of energy causing the guard to miss an attack as his short sword smashed into the ground.

"Damn it," Daniel snarled. But he had no time for this. Closing in on the line, Daniel slapped a hand on Omrak's back as he channeled a **Healer's Mark** into the Northerner's bigger body. At the same time, he extended his Gift into the man's body as he searched for the poison. Before Daniel could get a firm grip on the issue, Omrak strode forwards and broke contact, the Northerner's sword flashing out to sever the tongue tentacle that dragged the guard forward.

"Omrak…" Daniel snarled. But this was not the time to be concerned about things like that. By the side, Craig and the rest of his team outnumbered the Spligo who had attempted to flank the group on that side. As he entered battle, Craig triggered a Skill, stomping down hard with his lead foot and causing a ripple of power to flow out from the earth. It forced the Spligo to stumble, allowing Bjarne to swing his glowing blue weapon down and kill one of the monsters. Sumuhan strode forwards with his maul, ignoring a grasping tongue to close on his opponent and smash it into the ground. And from behind the group, Hjalmar somehow appeared, a pair of long knives digging into one monster's back just behind its jaws and nearly severing the head as his hands flashed.

Daniel turned away from that group, realising they did not need his help. On the opposite side, Rob had thrown out a pair of his enchanted ice orbs, creating a pair of angled ice walls that hampered the monster's approach. From above, arrows whistled and glowed before they struck the trapped monsters. Elisa's enchanted arrows seemed to burrow and burn as they struck while Tula's just multiplied, adding to the injuries of the group. But it was only Asin holding the group off, her pair of long daggers held before her as she defended the only exit.

"Damn it…" Daniel hesitated, torn between helping the Catkin and finishing his healing. He watched as Omrak had another strip of flesh torn from his arm, and the remaining guard stumbled to one knee, unable to stand further.

Even as he hesitated, the remaining caravan guards streamed in from behind. A few joined Daniel, the others Asin. As help arrived, it allowed Daniel a chance to move over to the original downed guard and drag him back while sending his Gift questing through the guard's body.

"Healer's Mark," Daniel muttered. He did not need to say the words, but in the confusion, Daniel did not have the time to care. Muttering the name allowed Daniel to focus his mind, trigger the spell formula, and force his Mana to flow in the manner it needed to cast the spell. At the same time, his Gift located the poison.

"Ugh…" Daniel shook his head, letting the man go after he finished pulling the body behind the new front lines. He eyed the battle again as he wiped his bloody hands on the ground, fingers already tingling from contact with the paralytic. As Daniel looked around, he realised that with the majority of the guard arrived, the fight had grown one-sided. Rather than join the battle, Daniel shifted his attention to healing the other guard. It was the least he could contribute.

***

"I told you to bring your people to the left," Craig said, standing before Daniel after the battle had been completed. The older Adventurer had dragged Daniel aside, behind a nearby caravan as he berated the healer.

"Omrak and the guards were falling," Daniel protested. "I thought it best to heal them."

"They only had to hold a short while more. If you had listened to me, we could have pinned the Spligo and finished them all. Instead, we've got the remnants of the pack running around," Craig said. "What good did your healing do?"

"Not much," Daniel admitted. "The poison just reapplies itself with a normal healing spell. Healer's Mark helps, but…"

"But it takes too long. I know," Craig said as he snarled. "That's why I wanted the Spligo dead. Your hammer would have been more useful."

"I know that now," Daniel said. If he had known the paralytic was not something he could heal easily, he might not have made the same decision. His Gift was not something he could use in the midst of combat. It required him to work intricate, microscopic changes in a body. It was part of the reason why it was so powerful—but it also required him to focus and keep constant contact. Anything beyond a quick assessment was outside of Daniel's ability. At least, presently.

"Then, let me remind you. I am in charge. You listen to my orders," Craig said. "Do you understand?"

"Yes," Daniel said, ducking his head.

"Good. Now, I've got a damn Ranger to set straight," Craig said as he turned.

"Set straight?" Tula said, appearing from the shadows. The Ranger in her dark camouflage outfit seemed to just appear from the darkness as she walked over. "About what?"

"I told you we should have killed them," Craig said, glaring at her. "Your indecision nearly got someone killed."

"You think so, do you?" Tula said emotionlessly.

"I know so."

"Follow me," Tula said and walked past the group. The Ranger brought the group towards the centre of the encampment where the drivers and Adventurers had the Spligo trussed up. "This the group you wanted me to attack?"

"Yes," Craig said.

"Count."

"What?"

"Count how many there are," Tula said. Craig, gaining an inkling of what was about to happen, tightened his lips but still turned to regard the trussed up corpses which were being skinned and butchered.

"Eleven," Craig said.

"How many adults?"

"Seven. Four children," Craig said. "And before you ask, there was at least another eight that escaped."

"Yes," Tula said and turned to look at Craig. She still spoke with the same monotone as she continued. "Not the same pack."

"Yes," Craig said, lips compressed before he sighed and bowed his head. "I'm sorry."

"Accepted. I was surprised too," Tula admitted. "There are too many Spligo packs. Someone has not been doing their job keeping this road clear."

"Could it be a migration?" Daniel asked.

"No. Spligo only travel when the food is scarce," Tula said. "Two packs with adults of this size indicate that a pack must have survived all summer last year."

"The local Guild should have been informed. And the local Lord. But there were no notices," Craig said, traces of anger in his voice.

Daniel winced and added checking route notices to the list of things he needed to do when taking on an expedition. It made sense, but it was not something that he had thought to do.

"I shall send a second notice when it is light," Tula said, gesturing around the still-buzzing campfire. "You should deal with this."

After the attack, no one seemed inclined to sleep. In the corner where the fight had happened, the wives of a pair of caravan guards stood, hands held out towards the blood-soaked ground. As they channeled their Skills, the blood and viscera floated and gathered into a ball in their hands before being deposited in a pail.

"Of course." Craig looked around and then, spotting Daniel, pointed at the healer. "Check if there are any additional injuries. Don't bottom your Mana out, but we should set up a rotating healing schedule." Daniel nodded but Craig was already stalking away in search of others to order around.

"You okay?" Daniel said, looking over to Tula who had let out a loud exhalation when Craig left.

"It's what we do," Tula said, the Ranger looking down at her feet for a time before she sighed. "But thank you for asking. Now, I need to speak with Sava."

Daniel nodded, watching the short Ranger head off. The healer shook his head and then turned away, searching for the aid station where he made his way over. To his surprise, Sumuhan was running the aid station along with one of the guards—working cloths, boiling water, and adding alcohol on wounds before wrapping them up with some pressed leaves.

"Ah, healer!" Sumuhan said. "Good. I have no stitched wounds close. If you have enough Mana…"

"I do," Daniel said. His eyes danced over the group, assessing damage before he moved to those most injured, laying on hands to begin casting **Healer's Mark.** The skill would heal forty-four hit points over the course of half an hour, patching the worse wounds together. For an experienced Adventurer like Daniel, it was only a fifth of his body's level-buffed health. But for the lower level guards, it would fix at least a fifth to a quarter of their health. In some cases, Daniel knew, he would have to cast the spell again, but none were in immediate danger.

When Daniel was done and had ordered more food to be brought over for the ravenous group of healing folk, he turned his attention to one of the sleeping figures. Laying a hand on the man's arm, he sent his Gift in to reassess the poison that still lingered in the body.

The poison itself was a foreign substance, an intruder in the body. It numbed muscle and slowed nerves, even as the flow of blood pulled and shuttled the poison to the liver where the organ broke the poison down. As an organic poison, the body could extract the poison in time, but it would take… four hours or so in this guard's case.

Good enough. Now that he had a better idea and feel for the poison, Daniel knew he could cleanse it from his own body with his Gift. Or, if he needed to, someone else's body. Though, considering his desire to keep his Gift secret, he would prefer to avoid that. For now, at least. Opening his eyes, Daniel removed his hand, only to be surprised by a new sight.

Skill Gained!
Poison Identification: Level 1 (02/100) +2

"Huh…" Daniel said. Well. That might be useful.

"Daniel, come. Eat!" Omrak called from his seat beside the fire. The big Northerner was sprawled out next to the fire, one leg bandaged and extended as he scoffed down a stick of meat. "The Spligo are quite good. Naturally spicy!"

"That's the counter-poison in the body actually," Elisa said, grinning up at the blond

Northerner. "The Beastkin pay good money for the glands."

By Elisa's side, Asin was nodding her head as she chewed on a stick as well, rubbing at a wound on her arm at times. Work done, at least for now, Daniel joined his friends. It seemed that no one was going to be getting any sleep tonight.

Chapter 8

In the morning the group broke camp, tired and yawning drovers and Adventurers taking to the road again. Just before the group left, Tula reappeared and spoke to both Sava and Craig in whispered tones. The group looked grim at whatever Tula said, but they did not share the knowledge with the rest of the caravan.

Instead, Tula strode over to the main road and released a trio of folded paper birds, the courier spells embedded within the messenger notes homing in on the Guild signature. From prior discussion, Daniel knew that this each paper cost a silver each. Before, Tula had used one of the many courier pigeons the caravan had brought to inform the local Guild about the initial pack of Spligo, but this time, it seemed that the Ranger was serious.

Over the next two days, the caravan caught sight of one other Spligo pack. This was the largest pack, with over nineteen members in all. The pack was lazing in a burrow-filled field, the alpha and other members of the pack standing and watching the trundling caravan on the road. Whether it was due to the bountiful food that the field offered or the distance, the distant pack chose not to follow the group, nor did Craig suggest it either.

Having rotated out of the lead position, Daniel was seated in the centre on a barrel with Uppulu, the dark-skinned Adventurer carefully working the edge of his spear with a whetstone. Rather than listen to the grating slide of stone and steel for another hour, Daniel spoke.

"What's going to happen to the Spligo?" Daniel said.

"Three packs, all birthing? If left unchecked, an outbreak. Soon, they'll have eaten or driven everything away and will attack the nearest village," Uppulu said. "A kill bounty will be placed on them. And the Guild will investigate the local Guild chapter."

"I don't understand how it could get this bad," Daniel said, lips compressing. "They must have realised this would happen."

"It might not be their fault," Uppulu said. "Just because a bounty is available does not mean Adventurers will take it. Or are allowed to take it."

"But that's what the local Lord is for, isn't it?" Daniel said. "He offers a bounty increase to attract Adventurers. Or deal with it himself with his personal guard."

Uppulu shrugged, but the driver spoke up. "We're moving through Lord Sade's lands now. He's eight years old."

"Eight?" Daniel said.

"Aye. Mother's the regent, but she's a Lady," the driver added. "Still no reason they didn't up the bounty, but I wouldn't expect them to be out here."

Turning his hammer over in his hand, Daniel eyed the empty enchantment slot as he mused about their comment. It was one weakness about the governing system. Brad's standing army was small and had its hands full dealing with Orc raids, larger bandit groups, and fortifying border garrisons. In-country problems like monster populations were dealt with by the local Lords and Adventurers. Most times, this worked, but occasionally gaps occurred.

Like this one.

Then again, was any system perfect? If there was one, Daniel did not know of it.

***

Two days later, Sava stood before the tired group, stomping around to alleviate the early morning chill. An unseasonably cold spring morning had left a rime of frost on everything and created a tense and grumpy atmosphere. When silence fell, the caravan master spoke.

"The Ranger says we are out of the Spligos' territory. Left it last afternoon," Sava said. A muted cheer erupted from the group, the tension of potential attacks at night and crowded sleeping conditions having depressed everyone further. "That means we're going to pick up the pace." Groans erupted from the group, but there were no protests. "We got three days to make up the time before we miss our meeting, and we're a day behind because of the slower pace. So, get ready for a long haul."

Clapping his hands together, Sava sent the group off and waved Craig and Daniel closer. The pair, along with Tula, joined the caravan master. Curious, Daniel wondered what additional news Sava had to share.

"I received word by courier pigeon this morning," Sava said, holding forth a small roll of paper. "The Guild has increased the bounty for the Spligo to double their normal rate. Including those we have reported." The Adventurers could not help but grin at the news, though Tula was unmoved. "As for the Lord, a royal investigator has been dispatched."

"Good," Tula said.

As the group dispersed to pass on the good news, Daniel spoke to Craig. "What's a royal investigator?"

"You don't know?" Craig said. Then he smiled wryly. "No reason you should, I guess. They're who deal with Lords and their ilk. If Lord Sade's regent does not have a good reason for their failure, I expect there will be a change of governance."

Daniel thanked Craig, heading off to report the latest news to his friends as the caravan began to roll out. As he walked, the healer could not help but muse about the widening world he was being exposed to. As an Advanced Adventurer, they were neophytes in the games of politics. Their actions, their choices could affect even Lords it seemed.

***

The rest of the day passed in short order. One day turned to the next. As the expedition continued into the wilderness, moving a clip that was only possible due to the passive movement Skills of the caravan master that bolstered the entire expedition, signs of civilisation faded. Even the occasional homestead or old, worn, and abandoned stone walls gave way to untamed wilderness. Distances between villages increased as the pioneers picked the best locations for making their new lives—finding waterways, untouched forests, and minerals to bolster their chances of success.

At each village, the expedition would stop and trade. At these times, the Adventurers would have time to rest and relax. Depending on the nature of the groups, the Adventurers would relax, catch up on sleep, gamble and drink or, in a few cases, explore the towns. Not that these villagers often had any real sites of interest, though the village heads would often have minor quests on offer.

"Devil Rats again?" Daniel groaned at the head villager's enthusiastic response. When he saw the man frown, he waved a hand. "Sorry. It's just that we've done the same quest for the last…"

"Three villages," Omrak said. "Do you not have other problems?"

"But we need the Devil Rats taken care of. They've already spoilt four of our grain bags," the head villager muttered.

"And we'll handle them. But surely it doesn't require all of us," Daniel said.

"Well, we don't have enough to pay for anything else."

"Just tell us," Omrak said.

"Upriver. The Belhu Crocodiles have been spawning and growing," the head villager said. "We try to keep their population contained."

"Perfect," Omrak said. "That is a more suitably glorious quest. I shall slay your crocodiles, skin their scales, and bring back their meat for all to feast upon. Come, Hero Craig. Let us begin!"

The older Adventurer looked between Omrak and his team and then back at his lazing group, some of whom were already half-drunk and shook his head. "No. I don't think so. You have fun."

"But the village needs us!" Omrak said.

"Needs you," Craig said. "There is not enough paid work. Nor would we want to deal with Devil Rats. Those are quests for Beginner Adventurers."

"But necessary work," Rob said, lips tightening. "Still, I feel that Asin would best be suited to that work."

Asin let out an inquisitive meow, though she fingered a throwing knife.

"Selkie. Water," Rob said, pointing to himself. Then he shifted the direction of his finger to point at Omrak. "Giant sword." Then to Asin. "Small daggers." As for Tula, the Ranger was resting on the roof of a caravan, enjoying the sun and a moment of rest. Of them all, the Ranger had done the most work, always ranging back and forth, scouting their route, and verifying problems.

"Daniel?" Asin said, prodding her friend.

"I was hoping to…" Seeing Asin's big eyes he sighed. "Help you. Fine."

"You will help us?" the head villager said, looking between the group. By this time, Craig had walked off.

"That is what we do!" Omrak said, clapping the head villager on the shoulder and staggering him. "Come, Friend Rob. We have monsters to slay!"

***

Daniel groaned, lifting another bag of grain and shifting it so that Asin could spot the rats. Devil Rats were large, almost the size of a large house cat. Due to the structure of their bones, it still meant they could squeeze their way through gaps, so not only were the pair of Adventurers searching for the rats themselves, they were looking for the way they had entered the grain barn. All of which consisted of moving the grain bags around.

As Asin poked around, Daniel rested against one stack of grain. "You just wanted help moving the bags, didn't you?"

Having verified there were no rats, Asin stepped back and flipped her throwing knife around. She looked at Daniel as she answered, offering him wide cat eyes. "No."

When Asin answered him, Daniel noted how her tail had frozen for just a brief second in its lazy swinging. "Sure."

"Friend. Together," Asin said, pointing between the two of them.

"Huh," Daniel said as he walked over to the next stack of grain bags. Thanks to their Levels, the act of carrying these grain bags was easier than he had expected. Sometimes, it was easy to forget that he had risen so many Levels in the short span of a year. He had 20 combined Levels. A Miner with 20 Levels could command a premium, his combined Skills and attributes making him twice to thrice as efficient as any beginner Miner. And those few Miners who managed to hit Level 40 were considered peak experts, individuals whose very presence guaranteed a good return for a company. In fact, many of these Miners would run their own companies or mining gangs. "We really have not hung out much alone, have we?"

"No," Asin said. She let out a satisfied purr as a Devil Rat darted out from beneath Daniel's feet as he shifted the next stack of grain sacks. As it went for the healer's feet, Asin threw her readied knives, the blades sinking deep into the creature's body, the wounds and lightning killing it immediately.

Daniel did not miss a beat, putting the grain sacks down and pointing to the hole in the ground they had located. "Found it."

"Maybe more."

"I know," Daniel said. Killing the Devil Rats was not hard for them at all. As Craig had mentioned, this was the kind of work that was best left to Beginner Adventurers—or a group of well-armed and ready villagers. Since there were no Beginner Adventurers around though, it was left to them to finish this. "Still. I bet there isn't another hole."

"Bet?"

"Stakes?"

"One silver."

"Done."

Motivated by the bet, Daniel started moving the grain sacks at a faster rate. The Catkin grabbed the Devil Rat, slinging the dead body outside for the peasants to deal with, but not before she retrieved her knife. After she re-entered, Asin hopped up on one sack and found a perch on a beam, the daggers still held in one hand as she did her little gymnastics routine. Even if they found the holes in the barn, they still had to find the monster's lair.

***

It was late evening before the party regrouped at the village square. There, an impromptu celebration was being conducted, a mark of gratitude for the caravan's arrival and the Adventurers' help. Beside the trio of cooking fires, three eight-foot-long crocodiles turned on spits, the centerpiece of the celebration. Beside the largest of the crocodiles, Omrak held court, waving a sawn-off back leg as a makeshift sword.

"Then, as Rob was about to be eaten by the monster, I swung my sword and lopped off its snout!" Omrak swung the drumstick down.

"I was in no danger," Rob said, sniffing. "I knew you were there. As if a stupid crocodile could catch a Selkie in the water."

"You're a Selkie? I thought you were seals?" A scrawny farmer said, looking at Rob with distrust.

"It is one of our forms."

"Forms? I thought you people were like the Beastkin," the same farmer said.

"No." Rob sniffed. "Unlike the Beastkin, we have two forms. We never gave up our heritage."

"That old lie?" Sumuhan who was seated a short distance away said with a growl. "You refused to aid Erlis when she needed it. And were thus cursed with having to choose each time."

"Lies!" Rob roared. He stepped forwards and pointed a finger at Sumuhan. "Lies that you Beastkin tell to explain why you gave up your real forms. Lies to explain why you are cursed to stand in those absurd forms."

"Say that again." Sumuhan stood up, his hand falling to the maul that rested against the chair he had been seated on. "Go on. Speak that lie again."

"You think I'm scared of you?" Rob said, snarling. From behind the Selkie, a pair of his floating spikes dropped from his jacket and floated up ahead of the Enchanter.

"Stop it. Both of you!" Craig said, placing himself between the pair. "What do you think you're doing?"

"He insulted us!"

"He's spreading his lies!"

"I don't care," Craig snarled. "This is a celebration. You are Advanced Adventurers. Act like it."

Daniel appeared beside Rob, prodding him in the side until the man stared at the Healer. He then pointed at the floating spikes before speaking. "Put the weapons away."

"Or else?"

"Or else Omrak will hit you with the drumstick, and then we'll roll you around in the mud until you calm down," Daniel said.

"Mud?" the fastidious Selkie shuddered. "Fine. But if he continues to pass on those lies..."

"You'll both shut up," Craig said, having overheard the conversation. Sumuhan growled but released his hold on his maul, sitting down.

Omrak, having watched the entire thing, just rolled his eyes and bit into his drumstick.

An hour later, once Daniel was certain that the group had settled and he had had Rob apologise to the village head, Daniel found Asin and poked her. The Catkin let out a disconsolate growl.

"What was that about?" Daniel said.

"Old stories," Asin said. "Anger."

"There's obviously a lot. I've never seen you and Rob get into it," Daniel said.

"Don't care," Asin said pointing at herself.

"It sounds like a rather important story though," Daniel said. After spending an hour of cudgelling his brain, Daniel had to admit that he actually did not know which story was true. In fact, he recalled hearing a few other stories about the creation of the Beastkin—mismanaged creations of Mages, forsaken children of one of the lesser gods… Even if the gods knew the truth, they did not speak it. Or, perhaps they did, and the priests refused to tell.

Asin sighed and then raised her hands. "Too many stories. Too long ago. No records. Gods tell lies." A rumble in the night sky had Asin look up and duck her head as she added. "Or are lied to. New gods don't know. Old gods don't talk. Or talk badly."

That, too, was true. Communication between the gods and the clergy was difficult, prone to miscommunication due to the difference in strength and status between the two. A god, a real god, was so far beyond mortals that only those with the highest Levels could sustain any real communication.

"So you don't care?"

"Make difference?" Asin said pointing at herself. "Asin. Cursed. Blessed. Still Asin."

Daniel opened his mouth and then shut it. True enough. If there was one truth to all their teachings, it was that life did not judge. It would break you and gift you in equal degree, whatever your beliefs. All you could do was go on.

"Food," Asin said, waving her empty plate. And then, having done talking philosophy, the Catkin walked off, leaving Daniel staring at the young Catkin's back.

Chapter 9

The Great Forest of Pirin stretched for miles as the group crested the next hill, a sea of green interrupted by a clearing dotted with the brown thatched houses of a village. The dirt road the expedition had been travelling on for the last two days, pushing through the mud and washed out gravel banks, led here—the village of Olyne. Olyne was the last outpost of civilisation for the Kingdom of Brad in this portion of the world and the last stop for the expedition before they entered the forest.

As the expedition crested the hill, Omrak walked over to Tula who stood by the side of the road, just past the hill so that she was not profiled against the sky. The Ranger was pensively biting her lips, her gaze locked on the village in a way that the Northerner had never seen before.

"Your home?" Omrak said as he came to a stop next to the short woman.

"Yes," Tula said. Surprisingly, she continued speaking, utterly unlike her normal close-mouthed attitude. "It's been three years since I was last here. It's not changed, not much. Another pair of houses, a bigger sawmill. Cut down more trees…"

"It's hard, home," Omrak rumbled. "I have not been home since I left four years ago."

"Four?" Tula said, surprised. She turned her head to look at Omrak, gaze drifting over the youthful giant's body.

"Yes. I left when I was fourteen," Omrak said, answering her unasked question. "It is customary among my people to consider a boy a man after his first kill. Mine was when I was thirteen. My mother refused to let me go until I was fourteen though." To the last sentence, Omrak continued to sound aggrieved. "But my father insisted that I be allowed to make my way."

"Do you regret it?"

"Regret what?"

"Leaving."

"No," Omrak said, shaking his head. "There is no place for me at home. My older brothers have the farm. When I have earned my coin and made my name, I shall return. I will buy the land below my brother's and raise sheep then. And then I will hire a farmhand to care for the sheep while I hunt in the mountains."

Tula snorted. "That's a nice dream."

"Aye. So, the village survives on lumber?"

"Lumber and beast harvest are the mainstays," Tula said. "But it's expeditions like this one that give us the money to improve."

Omrak nodded. It was not that different in his village. When you lived at the edge of nowhere, the community became used to creating the majority of their needs themselves. However, some things were just not possible to be created in a small village, and so the occasional traders and expeditions provided the necessities. In some ways, Omrak figured, this village was better off than his own for they had the guarantee of regular traders looking for monster parts. The highlands he came from had the same, but monsters were much rarer and much more dangerous.

"Ranger," Sava said as he hopped off his wagon, joining the pair as they watched the village. "Is there an issue?"

"No," Tula said.

"Good." Sava relaxed, looking around the forest and then upwards at the mid-day sun. "We should reach the village well in time. We will rest for three days and then begin the expedition proper."

Tula inclined her head at Sava's words.

The expedition master paused, looking from side-to-side nervously before he spoke. "The Esman Gorge-"

"Is dangerous," Tula cut in. "This is only an Advanced orange-rated expedition. We are not cleared to enter the gorge."

"If we only sent in some scouts…"

"No."

"Of course, Ranger," Sava said, nodding his head. Lips pursed, Sava considered before he spoke again. "Then, we will go to the Rybachly Lake."

"Acceptable. I'll verify conditions before we leave," Tula said.

Sava bobbed his head and then bade goodbye to the group, hurrying over to catch up with his wagon. The pair stood in silence for a bit, allowing more of the wagons and Sava to leave before Omrak spoke.

"What is the Sman Gorge?"

"Esman," Tula corrected. "A dangerous location. The Rangers have rated it as Advanced Green-Blue threat levels. But it also contains the eggs of the Nizhnye raptor which are highly prized for both beast taming and the kitchens."

Omrak nodded. "Well, it's good we're not going there then. I don't do well with birds."

"Most don't," Tula said. "Come, we should catch up. And I should let the village know we will arrive soon."

Once she had finished speaking, Tula took off, leaving Omrak to watch his friend disappear down the hill in the half-crouch, mile-eating lope that she did. In short order, he began to lose sight of her figure as her camouflaged clothing and the Ranger's ability to pick out minor dips and twists in the hill began to blend her figure in.

"What a wonderful day to be alive. Now, if there was a monster…"

"Don't jink us, you idiot!" Vivian, seated on a passing wagon, snapped at Omrak who offered her a wide grin in return.

***

It took the expedition the rest of the afternoon to reach the village, greet the titular village head, put up a temporary camp, and deal with curious villagers. By the time the expedition was settled, the sun had begun to set and campfires were being stoked. Having settled the expedition, Tula took off to finish the last of her duties, walking to the expansive treehouse with its ladder entrance that made up the Ranger outpost of the village.

She took hold of the simple rope ladder that led to the outpost, scurrying up the swaying contraption with practiced ease. Ranger outposts were the same the kingdom over where it was possible, built high to maximise sightlines and natural defences. That the village had then grown up around the outpost was not uncommon, leaving the giant tree and the Rangers within alone.

"Tula," the grizzled, salt-and-pepper Ranger who manned the outpost greeted the young Ranger the moment she arrived.

"2nd Class Apprentice Ranger Tula reporting in with an expedition from Silverstone," Tula said, striding over to the desk the Ranger manned. "Permission to begin, Ranger Luke?"

"Permission given, Apprentice Tula," Luke said.

Tula spoke quickly, detailing the trials of the expedition. As she spoke, the older Ranger made notes on sheaths of paper in a short-hand script, one that consisted of scribbled letters and hieroglyphs rather than full words. It was, in common parlance, Ranger script and what all

---

Rangers were taught to read from the beginning of their apprenticeship. Not only did it save on paper, it also allowed the Rangers to keep their secrets and pass them on, often in open view of others.

"And one nest of seven kappa seven miles north of waypoint eleven at the small lake shaped like a J," Tula said, finishing her report. "Not dealt with."

"Too far from the road for now," Luke said, pursing his lip. "But that nest could be a problem. I'll add a quest for it."

"Yes, sir," Tula said.

"If that's all," Luke said, and after Tula acknowledged it, he set his quill down and spread the papers apart to let them air dry. At that point, Luke broke into a wide grin, walking around the table to give Tula a big hug, spinning the diminutive Ranger around.

"Good to see you, sprout!"

"Mmpphfff…" Face pressed into Luke's chest, Tula struggled to speak and breathe.

"Ah, hush. I haven't seen you in years. To think, you're a 2nd Class Apprentice now!" Luke said, grinning wide. "Amazing."

Finally released after she stomped on Luke's foot, Tula growled at her old master before giving him a more comfortable hug. "You idiot. Are you still working here alone?"

"Ah, well, you know how it is," Luke said with a shrug. "Lots of talent, but little interest."

"Or their interest is disapproved of," Tula said, a trace of bitterness creeping into her voice. Luke snorted and smacked her on the shoulder.

"What, you want someone who hates the job working alongside you?" Luke said. "No. You know why we do things the way we do. Would you change it?"

"I'd…" Tula paused then her shoulders slumped in defeat. "I wouldn't. The Rangers take those who are called, not those who are interested."

"Exactly," Luke said. "So. The Rybachly Lake?"

"Yes. But he mentioned the gorge too," Tula said. Luke rolled his eyes at her words.

"Stay away. They had a good year since I took down the wyvern family that had been bothering the village," Luke said. "Be a few years before the Nizhnye raptors balance out. You might even see a few flying around if you're going to the lake."

"Then you best get me the details," Tula said. At Luke's gesture, the pair walked over to another table where a map of the surroundings was pinned down with small carvings situated across the map. As they reached the map, Luke began to point to each carving, detailing the threats each marking denoted. In turn, Tula listened intently, knowing that such information could make the difference between death and survival.

***

Late in the evening, Tula found herself outside the backdoor of a small house set near the edge of the village's wooden fence. The fence itself had seen numerous repairs since she had last been here, a constant requirement to ensure the village itself was safe. Of course, just a simple wooden barrier would never be enough, but that was what the numerous village dogs were for. One of which, having recognised an old friend, was butting up against Tula's hand, desperate for a scratch.

Tula sighed, staring at the imposing door again, and scratched the dog's ears, taking comfort in the loving comfort. Drawing a deep breath, Tula girded her courage and knocked. As her raised fist was coming down for the third time, the door flew open.

"Well, come in. Knocking as if you're a stranger. Really. And it took you long enough." The short, matronly woman within sniffed at Tula as she stalked back into the kitchen. "I kept your dinner warm, but it's so late, it's all be dried out."

"I'm sure it'll be fine, Mati," Tula said as she walked in and closed the door on the pitiful-looking dog. "Your food is always good."

"Not good enough to keep you here. Three years and we barely get a letter!" Tula's mother groused.

"I send one every time I can," Tula protested. "I can't help it if there are no traders when I'm on an expedition."

"Bah! You should stop with all this expedition nonsense. Be a proper Adventurer if you have to go run around," Tula's mati said. "At least you sent letters properly when you were doing that Dungeon."

"You know I hate being stuck in one place," Tula said, putting hands on her hips.

"Har! As if I wouldn't know why my own baby left me."

"Mati!"

"Oh, fine, fine. You have your life to live. Not as if anything I say has ever made a difference. Not as if your sister isn't happy being married to Laust and has their third kid on the way, no?" Tula's mati continued to mutter as she spooned the simple stew into a bowl and then added slices of a roast and grease-fried potatoes to a plate, all of which was placed before Tula.

"A third child?" Tula said, stabbing one of the pieces of meat. "Already?"

"Yes, a third. The other two are growing up good, though we had a scare with young Anders last winter when he caught a cold. Nearly lost him…" Successfully diverted, Tula's mati began to detail the trials and travails of village life.

In turn, Tula listened with one ear open, garnering some details that had not been passed on in their sporadic letters. It was comforting to be at home, eating familiar, too-greasy food. It was a trial too as her mother's constant, loving complaints rained upon her. Still, as she speared another potato, the Ranger found the knot in her shoulders relaxing. Home was where you could always come back, even if you never did want to.

Chapter 10

"It really was a very nice village," Daniel said. Two days later, the expedition was on the move. As they were headed into the overgrown forest, the expedition was moving mostly on foot with the supplies placed on a half dozen pack horses detached from their wagons. The Adventurers were all carrying their own goods, most of which were stored in their **Inventory** space. Of course, Merchants and Traders had their equivalent Skills, though many preferred to use Skills like **Lightened Load** or **Perfect Fit** that maximised the amount of space their conveyances and bag could carry. After all, a single carriage was many times more expansive than an Adventurer's **Inventory**.

In reply to Daniel, Asin let out a low purr.

"And Tula's mother was very nice. A bit wordy, but very nice," Daniel continued. Another purr from Asin. "She even gave us a warm meal for today."

"Mmmmrrmmm."

"So. Is that what mothers are like?" Daniel asked. Since his own had died so long ago he could not even remember her face, and his dad when he was a child, the entire 'homely' atmosphere was a bit of a shock to the Adventurer.

"Some."

"We are in the forest now. Quiet," Bjarne who was walking alongside the pair of Adventurers said.

Daniel flashed Bjarne a quick smile before he stayed silent. Not that he understood the reason. Between the horses, their tack and baggage and the tromp of the numerous members of the expedition, it was not as if their little group was silent. Even if they had left behind a large number of the merchants who had no talent at moving silently, they were not a quiet group. Any monster that wanted them would find them easily enough.

Then again, it was probably to allow the guards to hear any potential ambush group first rather than for the team to not attract attention. Or a little of both, since the noise from conversations between the tens of members of the expedition would travel even farther.

Coming that far in his thoughts, Daniel had to admit there were good reasons to be quiet. It was not as if the forest was safe. Monster attacks were pretty much a given. The number of plants that were known to be dangerous were high too – from hanging vines that shifted towards body heat and wrapped their prey up to poisonous groves of trees that would lull travellers to sleep under their boughs.

For all that, there was beauty too. As an ex-Miner, Daniel was more familiar with the depths of a mountain than he was with the expanse of the forest, but he had seen his fair share of them. Yet, the Great Forest of Pirin had managed to live up to its name. Brilliant, lush vegetation abounded, and flowers the size of his head gave off the most delightful floral scents along with fruits the size of fists. By his side, Asin had located and was peeling apart the skin of mangsteen—a mutated plant similar to a mango but with a thicker, furred skin. The flesh of the mangsteen came off in firm slices as Asin used her claws to great effect, popping the sweet flesh into her mouth without pause.

"Could be poisonous," Daniel muttered to his friend.

Asin sniffed, then pointed to Sumuhan. **"Poison detection."**

"Really?" Daniel said, eyebrow rising. That was an interesting and unique Skill. It was not one that was of great use among Dungeon-delving Adventurers. Smart Adventurers just carried a lot of poison resistance potions and assumed that most things would be poisoned—but out here, he could see how it could be useful. Of course, the question then became, what kind of skill was required to practice to get that kind of Skill?

Asin's answer was to proffer an unpeeled fruit to Daniel. There was a brief hesitation before Daniel took the fruit in hand and pulled his knife out to peel it out. Of course, he did not stop from regarding their surroundings, but right now, the pair of them were not on guard duty.

The mangsteen was slightly chewy and extremely sweet, the taste of the fruit filling his mouth. Each bite refreshed the taste, a lovely relief as he scanned the area. On occasion, Daniel heard the chirping of birds in the distance and the never-ending buzz of insects. But overall, it was a peaceful walk—so far. Not that Daniel expected otherwise —this close to the village, most large predators would have learnt to avoid the group. No. The real danger would only arise later, in the true depths of the forest.

***

Late at night, Rob crawled out of the humid tent he had been attempting to fall asleep in, groaning as he straightened up. As an Enchanter, his attributes mostly focused on his Intelligence and Willpower. Sure, as an Adventurer, he had slotted a few of his extra Skill points into Constitution, but it was not as if it was even of secondary importance. Which meant that the constant, never-ending walk that had been this day left him with a constant ache in his feet and bum. Now, rather than a comfortable bed to sleep in, he had to sleep in a humid, stuffy tent with a mildew bedroll.

"Either be wet or dry," Rob grumbled to himself. Hiding a yawn, the Selkie limped over to the nearest fireplace. "This humidity is ridiculous."

"I agree," Vivian said. "Wish I had a cooling and drying spell."

"Mmmm…" Rob's eyes tightened in thought. After a brief moment of consideration, the Selkie shook his head. "Not worth it. You'd have to use at least four anchor points and a central enchantment…"

"You're the Enchanter, right?" Vivian said. "I'm Vivian. We haven't had much chance to talk."

"Yes, I am. And you're the sorcerer," Rob said.

"You didn't sneer."

"Should I?"

"Most mages do."

"I'm not a mage," Rob said. As Vivian continued to stare inquisitively at him, Rob relented and added, "Selkies do not have many Mages. Most who have the ability and desire to learn in a structured format become Enchanters like me. Those who are magically inclined but less academically inclined are either Shamans or Sorcerers like you."

"Oh," Vivian said. "I didn't know that. But…"

"Ask if you intend to ask."

"Why Enchanters?" Vivian gestured to Rob's body. "When you're, you know-"

"Transformed."

"Right, that. You can't really, you know, carry your enchantments with you, can you?"

In answer, Rob flicked his fingers. From behind and around his robes, his enchanted spikes floated, twisting and hovering beside his body. Vivian's eyes widened and then narrowed as she considered the implications.

"But auric enchantments…"

"Can be created to blend and transform with Selkie skins," Rob said. "The gestures and incantations of a Mage are much more complicated and constraining. Enchantments, properly created enchantments, allow you to layer multiple effects. An Enchanter, given enough time and resources, can face any threat." Vivian's lips curled up slightly, watching Rob get impassioned. When Rob realised what he was doing, he flushed and then ducked his head. "Sorry."

"No need. It was kind of cute."

Rob turned even redder, looking away from the Sorcerer. "And you? Why did you choose to be a Sorcerer?"

"Money," Vivian said simply.

"Money?"

"Spell books are expensive. Magic lessons are even more expensive. I learned enough from my… well… I learned enough to cast my first spell. And that was good enough for me to clear the first floor of the Alanora Dungeon. Then I leveled and I got the Skill option for Sorcerer as an option and, well, it would give me a second spell." Vivian shrugged. "I needed to do the second level, and no one wanted a Mage with one spell. But a Sorcerer with two? That was useful."

Rob inclined his head in thanks for her story. All too often, the Dungeons were the dumping ground of towns. It was not a direct policy, but if you were poor, hungry and had the registration fee, the Dungeon shone as a beacon of hope. There were even predators, money lenders, and trainers, who preyed on the desperate, teaching and lending just enough to allow their victims to enter the Dungeons. High interest rates meant that these unlucky few often found themselves forced to delve deeper and deeper, faster than their barebone Skills could keep up with. In this way, overpopulation and homeless problems fixed themselves, especially in some of the more ruthless cities.

As the pair fell silent and Rob tried to hide a yawn, their attention was drawn to a light that flitted towards them. It bobbed and weaved, glittering in all the hues of purple and blue, a shifting living violet and changing sky. In short order, a second light joined it, the flaming red of a rose to the softer, kinder colours of a sunset. Then a third, but this one glittering with the shades of gold and ripened grain. As more and more lights appeared, joining the first few, the once dark campground became lively and bright.

"Shit… they're monsters," Rob said, realisation dawning on him when he shook himself awake from being beguiled. He reached a hand out for one of his enchanted balls, intending to use the area effect attack to deal with the monsters. Only to have a hand fall on his.

"Stop," Tula said.

"What…?"

"They're harmless."

"Are you sure?" Rob said, doubt in his voice. In his experience, anything this beautiful, this enthralling, was just a prelude to an attack.

"The sylphina angels are natural creatures, morphed by being in the Great Forest. This variety only appears here, in this forest," Tula said. She reached out, and one of the lights alit on her hand, its wings flapping on her fingers. "Their lights are entirely benign." Tula paused, her voice dropping as she stared at the butterflies before she added, "There used to be hundreds, tens of hundreds of them when I was younger. A random mutation caused by Mana. But, it's a benign mutation, a useless one. And it makes them easier to eat, so…"

"They've been dying off," Vivian said, her voice soft and sad. Tula looked over to the other girl who had her hand out, staring at the butterfly that had landed on her hand, which shone and glittered so beautifully. And fatally.

"Yes," Tula replied softly. So softly that Rob could barely hear her.

Together, the three watched the butterflies as they flitted around the camp in silence. The guards had been warned by Tula, and so none of them took action. But soon enough, too soon it seemed, the butterflies took off and left the campsite in search of sustenance. Leaving behind a trio of Adventurers that had seen something beautiful and tragic. Something ephemeral.

"Rob?" Vivian said, looking at the Selkie.

"Nothing," Rob said, turning away from the women and wiping at his face. Stupid human form. He waved a hand to them, waving goodbye to the group. Not because he was ashamed of his tears.

Not necessarily. But a part of him remembered the clouds of jellyfish, the beautiful, deadly display that they signified. And it ached to be back home. To feel the ocean water on his skin, to float and swim and dance. He knew he could not. Not now. Perhaps not ever.

And so, Rob crawled into a too hot, too humid tent rather than admit it.

***

A day and a half later, the group reached the river that fed into the Rybachly Lake. A glacier-fed river from the mountain range of Tatra, the river would eventually reach the sea, though not before merging with another river. Around the cold, cobalt green river, alder and willows grew, the willows drooping so deep that they often touched the water, shading the riverside.

"Ranger?" Sava said when Tula made her way over to the group.

"There's a suitable spot ahead to refill water and rest for lunch," Tula said. Sava nodded, and in short order, the group made their way over to the small, natural beach that Tula had located. As the porters and designated cooks got campfires ready, the Adventurers took turns watching the river and the forest before moving to refill their water bottles.

As Daniel kneeled beside the river with his bottle, he kept a close eye on the rippling liquid. One of the most common enchantments that any long-term traveller purchased was an enchanted water bottle to cleanse the life-giving liquid from all but the dirtiest and most polluted of water sources. Outside of mundane concerns like pathogens, the greater concern were the numerous parasites that lived in the water. Many were so small they were invisible to the naked eye, but they could, once lodged in a stomach intestine, grow and multiply. At first, they would just take nutrients, but in time, they would grow to such an extent that they would begin to eat their way out of their host. Many of these monsters were even more powerful than normal monsters due to their special growth circumstances. As a Healer, Daniel had dealt with more than one of those cases, the most vivid being the time when he had assisted in the cutting open of a nine-year-old child to extract a squirming, multi-legged monster. It was only with the layering of multiple healing spells and a touch of his Gift that they had managed to save the girl.

Cold water rushed over his now numb fingers, and Daniel woke from his memories. As he capped the bottle and ascertained that the enchantment was still working, the Adventurer wondered why the horrors he saw as a Healer were more vivid, more urgent than those he gained while Adventuring. Was it a simple case of being able to smash away the monsters in real life, while the horrors of old age, accidental amputations, and twice-infected injuries could, at best, be healed via spell and Gift. And in most cases, could just be bandaged, dosed, and slowly treated.

"Incoming!" Craig's rough voice broke Daniel's musings. A motion slipped the water bottle into his inventory as Daniel dropped his hand to his enchanted hammer and unslung his shield. Enchanted perhaps, but thus far, he had yet to 'capture' a second monster. The low probability of capture made the weapon less than ideal.

As Elisa and Sumuhan arrived wielding bow and javelin, Daniel followed their gazes to the threat that Craig had spotted. Looking like distorted logs, dark-brown with flashes of green, the monsters could only be differentiated by the lazy flap of fins. As if realising that their surprise attack had been found out, the monsters sped up, fins making waves as the lead monster yawned.

Long, angular snouts widened as jaws detached farther and farther apart, serrated teeth on a slim, fish-like body. As fins continued to flap, Daniel realised that those backfins were part of stumpy, muscular legs, ones that kicked out now to bring the monster closer.

Adult Cipactli (Level 16)
HP: 170/170

Information flashed before Daniel's eyes as he correctly viewed the monster. Removing his shield, he backed away from the water slightly as the others began firing. An arrow zipped past, skittering off scales before a heavier javelin landed, piercing the hide of the lead monster. It stuck in the flesh briefly before the cipactli rolled over, dislodging the javelin and allowing its compatriots to overtake it.

In the shallows now, the cipactli got their legs beneath them and thrust upwards, throwing themselves into the sky. As a formerly oblivious porter screamed in fright, arrows and an enchanted spike flew out to meet the monsters.

"Back off! Let the Adventurers handle them," Sava ordered, chivying his people back.

Daniel grunted, rushing over to the pair that had managed to land without doing any damage. On the ground, the cipactli were a weird mixture of crocodile, fish and toad, brown in nature. What he had once thought to be the edges of scales opened in the air, revealing numerous, screaming mouths.

"Spitting poison!" Tula called out in warning.

Not a moment too soon, for the numerous mouths began to emit squirts of liquid. Daniel brought his shield in front of him as he crouched behind the wooden protection. Even as the liquid fell to the ground, Daniel's eyes watered from the poisonous gases that it emitted.

"Take them from a distance!" Craig called out.

Behind Daniel, the sound of the final cipactli landing onshore resounded. But he had no time for this, as the monster that had targeted him decided to rush the Healer.

"Why me?" Daniel shouted in anger and frustration as he backed off. Since they had been moving at speed, Daniel had elected to only wear the breastplate of his plate armor; the rest of his armor was from his leather set. It was entirely mismatched, but mismatched was better than dying of sweltering heat while clad in stuffy and heavy iron plate. Perhaps on his next Level Up, he would finally get a chance to pick up a much needed 'comfort' Skill for heavy armor. Until then, he had to compromise between defense and practicality.

Hunkered behind his shield, Daniel occasionally glanced around the edges of it. Each time, he narrowly avoided being sprayed by the poison, forcing the Healer to constantly back off. As a foot came down on a root, Daniel hesitated as he regained his balance. That momentary pause was enough for the cipactli to launch itself, tiny clawed fins scrabbling at the edges of his shield and pulling it down.

Over the edge of his shield, Daniel met the gaze of the cipactli, deep-set, beady eyes filled with malevolence staring back at the Healer. The monster opened its mouth, breaking eye contact as it readied itself to hurl poison directly at Daniel.

145

Reacting on instinct, Daniel threw his helmeted head forwards, smashing the monster's jaws shut on its own poison spray as he head-butted the creature.

Unfortunately, not all of the forceful spray was contained, the edges of the liquid and vapours assaulting Daniel's eyes. In the corner of his eyes, in his mind, a notification flashed.

You are poisoned.
-5 HP per second for 4 minutes.
You are partially blinded.

The Healer snarled as he staggered backwards, punching out with his trapped hand as he called forth his **Shield Bash** Skill. The cipactli, held forth on the shield was thrown forwards, losing its grip but not taking much damage from the attack. It did allow Daniel to back off and stumble to his knees, his hammer hand wiping at his watering eyes. Pain pulsed through his face, entering from the nerves around his face and his breathing tract, flashing downwards and forcing Daniel's body to clench as it fought off the poison.

A meaty thunk ahead of Daniel reminded the Healer that the fight was still on-going. As Daniel tried to rise, a hand dropped on his shoulder.

"Stay, Healer. Heal thyself. I shall guard you," Uppulu said, his voice coming from beside Daniel. "You will be needed soon."

Jerking his head down in assent, Daniel forced himself to calm down and catalog the damage. Burning skin and nerves, so not a numbing poison. It seemed to see through the skin. The way it hurt his throat showed that it was also easily dispersed through the air. A hand conjured up his water bottle, and Daniel tilted his head up as he poured the water over his face, washing away some of the poison.

Poison effect and duration reduced
Partial blindness reduced.
-3 HP per minute

"Use water. Wet cloths over mouth," Daniel croaked out, offering advice. As he blinked away tears, Daniel squinted through blurry eyes to gauge the fight. Of the two cipactli, one lay on the ground, skewered by a javelin and twitched, unable to move. The second one still fought, but its back leg had been smashed and a trio of arrows stuck out from its side, slowly killing it. As for the former lead monster, its corpse floated down the river.

Even as Daniel struggled to his feet, he watched as Vivian sent a dart of flame into an open mouth, searing it shut and causing the monster to thrash in distress. The distraction was enough for Craig to finish the creature off, jumping forwards to impale it with his weapon.

"Or, you know, kill it," Daniel said. He took a mouthful of water and gargled, before spitting out the contaminated fluid and taking a deeper drink. He felt a pulse of pain again as the poison ate at his nerves, but he shook it aside as he searched for the injured.

There.

"Clean the wounds with water,' Daniel ordered the man as he staggered forward. As Uppulu grabbed his arm, Daniel made note of another side effect—balance disruption. "Or, wherever he was hit…"

"Daniel?" Rob said, approaching from the side. "Is there anything I can do?"

"No," Daniel said, shaking his head. "Time. That's all of it. I think."

"Healing spells?" Sava said. He looked worried, seeing as the other two injured were merchants like him, with low health in comparison to the tougher Adventurers.

"Wait," Daniel said. He coughed, turned aside and spat a glob of blood and saliva out before he took another step forward. "Healing spells with poison heals around the poison. Sometimes it lengthens the duration of damage."

"Then what do we do?" Sava asked.

Rather than answer Sava, Daniel sank down next to the pair of injured merchants. Hands moved, shifting the bodies around, his gaze tracking over the reddened skin, his breathing shallow and fast. He frowned, realising the pain in his throat and chest was not just from the initial assault.

"Move them. Us. Poison in the air," Daniel said. It was already fading, the concentration too low to do more than irritate the healthy and uninjured. But for those that had been already poisoned, it was unlikely to do much good. Better to leave.

"Ranger!" Sava called out.

"This way," Tula said as she appeared from within the forest. Unlike the rest of them, the Ranger had been off scouting, searching for the best route.

In short order, the injured were being moved aside, carried away rather than being allowed to walk. Daniel refused additional help, instead staying next to the injured. Even as he walked— one hand on the improvised stretcher, the other held by Uppulu—Daniel sent his Gift into himself.

Poison. It was easy to sense, easy to find. It was a nasty poison, but luckily, one that the body could break down. Already, Daniel could see how the kidney and liver were hard at work, taking the traces of the poison that it encountered and counteracting it. Luckily, the poison was neutralising itself too as its concentration reduced. Daniel briefly debated and then sent his Gift deeper into himself, feeling a memory disappear as he cleared out the damage around his eyes.

____

"So, Healer. Prognosis?" Sava asked. Daniel tilted his head to the side, eyeing the way Sava stroked a blue bottle by his side.

"Time," Daniel said. "Two to four hours for the poison to clear. They should survive. Once the poison is gone, I'll cast healing spells on them all. They'll need food and drink afterwards, and preferably, rest."

Sava clapped Daniel on the shoulder in thanks before he made his way over to the injured, passing words of comfort to the pair. Uppulu, having listened to the conversation, glanced at Daniel.

"You're walking a little better," Uppulu said.

"Healed myself," Daniel said. Then, at Uppulu's raised eyebrow, he continued. "I know my body. I can guide the spell easier inside me, because it's me."

"Interesting. Can all Healer's do that?" Uppulu asked.

"Yes. Outside of our bodies, we have to rely on the spell itself to do the healing. At least, at my level." Daniel paused, then smiled ruefully. "Better healers, real Healers, they're trained to slowly take apart healing spells and manipulate the portions. In time, they can make even a simple healing spell twice to thrice as effective."

"Interesting. So, that is why the more experienced Healer's charge more, for the same spells."

"Mostly. There's also regeneration rates to worry about," Daniel said. That, as always, was the greatest concern. A small spell was no issue and could be regenerated in ten or twenty minutes. But the sick and injured were never-ending and Mana pools were not. Eventually, even 'small' spells would drain a Healer entirely, making them unable to cast the more powerful, more effective spells. And so, many Healers would price their smaller healing spells as a portion of the more powerful spells to justify their use.

"Watch your step," Uppulu warned Daniel who grunted his thanks and stepped over a rather large fecal deposit. Saving his breath, Daniel stayed silent as he followed along, mentally charting the spell and any potential adjustments he could make. While he might not be a true Healer, he did have some knowledge of the spell and the poison. A little tweak here and there would help.

Chapter 11

Three days after the attack from the cipactli, the group reached the lake. The Rybachly Lake was large and a placid blue, filled on one side with lotus pads and the other by sheer cliffs that walled off the cliff itself. Having arrived a short distance from the river, Tula led the group towards a clearing a distance from the lake, allowing them to rest without potential additional attacks. Over the course of a few days, between layered spells and rest, the injured had fully healed up.

Once the camp had been set and protective wards and traps laid out, Sava called a meeting to lay out the goals for the group for the next few weeks. Using the lake as a simple source of water, they would also spend the time hunting monsters and animals that came to drink from the lake. The harvesters would swing out around the rivers and the camp, searching for rare herbs and plants to bring back.

"Lastly, Prek. You and Ger set-up the boat. You'll be supplementing our provisions with your catch, so make sure to catch a lot,' Sava said.

"You have a boat?" Omrak said, looking around the campsite.

"In my storage," Prek said, an older chubby merchant that had kept up with the group surprisingly well. "**Small - Fisherman's Dock** lets me store a boat to safeguard it."

"You're a Fisherman?" Craig said, frowning as he looked over Prek.

"Level 14," Prek said proudly.

"If he spent more time selling, he'd be a higher level Merchant," Sava said, shaking his head.

"Ah, but that's what you're there for, right?" Prek said and sniffed. "Anyway, who wants to deal with all the hassle?"

"And that's why you're still stuck," Sava said with a sniff. "Now, for the Adventurers. We're going to need to split your parties up. We have three groups, of which we'll need you to guard, not including the base camp. So, here's what we are thinking…"

Daniel leaned in, his ears perking up as he listened to Craig's proposal. For the hunters, Sava wanted the long-range Adventurers, those with bows and magic, to hunt and slay their prey in short order. Outside of that, the melee fighters would be split relatively evenly among the gatherers and the base camp with only a single Adventurer on the boat.

"And that'd be myself, Rob, Omrak, and Sumuhan on the boat then in turns," Craig said.

"I fear that is not wise, Hero Craig," Omrak said.

"Why?" Craig said.

"I know not how to swim," Omrak admitted.

"Oh. Huh. Umm… Daniel?" Craig said.

"I can take over. I'll need to change out of my armor, but it should be fine," Daniel said.

"Good," Craig said, looking over to Sava to confirm the merchant was happy before they agreed. Rob, seated beside Omrak, was frowning and prodding his friend.

"How can you not know how to swim?" Rob said incredulously.

"Because I never learnt." Seeing that Rob was still astounded, Omrak continued. "I did live in the mountains, no?"

"But, lakes? Rivers?"

"Ice cold. You dipped in and washed, but you did not swim."

"It's not that cold."

"For you perhaps," Omrak pointed out. "But we are not Selkie. We do not have fur or your resistance to cold."

"But…"

Before Daniel could continue eavesdropping on the conversation, Craig had made his way over to him. "For the first day, I would prefer to be in the camp to deal with unexpected issues. We'll need a larger number in base camp on the first day." Tula appeared beside the pair, looking between the two. "Yes, Ranger?"

"I'm going to scout," Tula said. "No farther than two miles from the camp or the lake. Stay on the surface of the lake only."

"Sure," Daniel said.

Craig grimaced, but he gave her a short nod in agreement. Once the pair had nodded, Tula walked over to Sava to confirm her intentions before leaving the encampment, bow on her back and a small pack attached. Daniel frowned, watching as she left before he shook his head. If he was going to be with Prek today, he best remove his armor.

***

The boat that Prek pulled out when they found a suitable beach was a large rowboat, big enough to have space for three to sit on their own benches. Daniel was sent to the middle where the oars were after he volunteered that, yes, he did indeed know how to row. Once they were ready, the three pushed off, Prek directing Daniel to a suitable location that was shaded by an overhanging cliff-face.

"Right, just keep us here for now and we'll get to it. What do you think, Ger, crab traps?" Prek said as he pulled out the fishing net from where they had been stowed. In short order, the fisherman was checking the net over, readying it to be tossed in.

"Crab traps," Ger agreed. Even as he spoke, he was readying the crab traps by placing in pieces of offal, attaching them via hooks to the bottom of the trap before tossing the trap into the water with an easy over-hand toss. To Daniel's surprise, Ger actually let go of the rope, allowing the entire trap to fly away. Only when a small float bobbed up later, showing where the trap was located, did Daniel relax.

In the meantime, Prek had finished his preparations and stood up, balancing easily on the lightly rocking boat before he cast the net into the water. He let the rope play out in his hand as the net sank, having expertly sprung open as he threw it.

Daniel watched all this with interest, though he occasionally cast a suspicious look around for additional threats. Nets were something they had considered using against the imps, but experience had shown that tossing nets and having them hit was more difficult than they had thought. In the end, the use of the rockbow had been a lot more convenient. Still, there might be little tips to the casting of these weapons that could be learnt from watching someone this experienced.

In short order, the fishing group hauled up the first of their haul. With numerous crab traps situated close by, Prek ordered Daniel to row away from those traps, working the edges of the self-imposed boundary to find new fish. The haul was bountiful. So much so that the group spent as much time sorting and storing the haul as they did fish.

"Another Skill?" Daniel asked curiously as Ger made another fish disappear from his hands.

"**Fisherman's Haul**," Ger confirmed. "Prek used his storage Skill on the boat. I used mine on the haul. Works best that way."

___

"I can see that," Daniel said. "I could store some if you want?" His **Inventory** ability was limited in size, but outside of his some ancillary weapons and survival equipment, Daniel had deposited all his Adventuring equipment at base camp, leaving him with a chest worth of free space.

"Nah. Adventurer **Inventory's** don't keep the taste right. Too warm," Ger said.

"Hold up on that thought, Ger. If we let him keep the camp's supply, we could store more for sale," Prek said.

"Fair enough. Alright, you store the ones I give you," Ger said. In short order, Ger handed Daniel a pink-striped fish, about the size of his arm. Daniel watched the creature's mouth move as it gasped for air before he shrugged and willed the fish away.

It was another two hauls before their first major delay occurred. The net when it came up was broken, a large hole in one side showing where a more aggressive fish had made its escape. Neither fishermen were particularly surprised, and Prek took to fixing the net immediately, making twine appear from a small pouch by his side.

"Might as well drop the anchor here," Ger said as he hunted for, and found, a pair of fishing rods. "We'll be here a bit until Prek has fixed the net."

"What are you doing?" Daniel said after he had dropped anchor. By the time he was done, Ger had baited and sunk the fishing hook in the water before offering the rod to Daniel.

"Line fishing. Might catch something good with the lures I got," Ger said.

"But…" Daniel paused.

"We'll see and sense any trouble long before it arrives," Ger said, tapping his head with one slimy finger. "**Sea Sense.** We both have it."

"Then, why'd you need me for?"

"Can't always run. And nice to have a third pair of hands to row," Ger replied as he cast his own rod. After playing with the rod a little, he added. "Relax. Ours is the easiest job there is. And before you ask, sure, we have a spare net. Have two. But I'm already two-thirds full. Once we add the crab haul, we'd be done in a day. No real point hurrying with the haul. Better to get something good than just filling up the nothing, you know?"

"Not really," Daniel admitted. This seemed like a different way of doing things, but the Adventurer had to admit, fishing on an expedition probably had much different constraints to when he mined. A small mining operation still consisted of tens of Miners. "So, now what?"

"Now, we fish," Ger said with a grin as he leaned back. From his side, Ger pulled out a bottle, popping the sealed cork top and taking a swig. Even a foot away, Daniel could smell the alcohol in the bottle. "Drink?"

"No. I think… no." Daniel shook his head. His job was to keep the pair safe. Though, as Daniel looked longingly as the pair shared the bottle, passing it between each other, he wished he was not so uptight. Just a little. But, expeditions were dangerous. And he would not see another injured because of his carelessness.

***

Back at the camp, Asin slunk around the small depression that the group had chosen for their campground. The Beastkin bounced off the set of collapsed stone, climbing quickly to ascend to the top of the worn stone to take her place as the camp's guard. At the top of the destroyed masonry, she considered the steep drop that had resulted before fishing in her belt pouch. In short order, she had laid out a simple string and bell warning system and then added a second, nastier trap just over the edge of the cliff. Satisfied, the Catkin then dropped back down a few feet.

In short order, Asin found a comfortable seat just beneath the topmost portion of the tumbled masonry, a short distance from her trap. Having made herself comfortable, Asin unslung Daniel's crossbow and placed the quiver beside herself before squirming down to take her watch.

Ranger approved or not, Asin was not entirely sure she agreed with the choice of campsite. Sure, the depression and the strange tumbled masonry made for an easily defensible location—there were only two easy entrances to the campsite without clambering over bramble-filled and crumbling masonry. That made the campsite highly defensible and also made sure that the glow of their campfires at night would not reflect as far. Along with the trees that covered the edges of the clearing, they were relatively well hidden.

But it also meant that there were only two major ways to run away. That seemed like a horrible idea to Asin, but as the Catkin considered the issue she sighed.

"Beast." She chuffed out, realising the issue. She thought of mortal enemies, of sentient monsters like the cunning Kobolds or the lizardmen. They ganged up, ran away, laid traps and fought smart. But for Tula, her greatest concern was not sentient monsters but beasts. Predators that might be aggressive and even have some low cunning but not the sentient ability to hunt and plan. In that case, two exits were probably significant.

It still did not sit well with Asin, though. The Catkin eyed their surroundings, absently tracing a claw over the ruined stone. For a brief moment, interest sparked in the Adventurer as she looked down at the hard stone. Even now, centuries later, the stone refused to come apart under her sharp nails. What had been built here? A former outpost of the Empire? Centuries ago, the Empire had fallen. But before that, it had spread its tendrils through monster-infested lands, the height of civilization.

Human civilization. Asin's lips curled slightly as she chuffed out the unhappy thought. Old history, but it was only after the fall that the Beastkin had scrambled upwards. Not that the history of the Beastkin had been all one-sided. At one time, they had even been the foremost members of the army.

Old stories. Dead stories.

Asin sniffed, discarding the useless thoughts. The here and now was important. And the future. The past was dead and could stay that way. Better to consider what she could do to make sure they were not dead too—if the Ranger's expectations were not met.

***

Three days later, Daniel had to admit, the expedition had been off to a weird start. Not only was their time significantly more peaceful than he had expected, the number of battles the group had to contend with could be counted on a single finger. That is, if you didn't count the hunts.

"Is this normal?" Daniel asked Tula that night when she came back.

"Is what?" the Ranger replied, staring up at the beefy Adventurer.

"The lack of combat," Daniel explained.

"If you've got a Ranger, yes," Tula said with a sniff. "Our job is to get you back alive. Which means finding the right routes, having you camp in the right areas, and then setting up traps and bait to keep predators away."

"Is that what you've been doing?" Daniel said, surprised. "I thought you were scouting."

"That is scouting. Ranger scouting," Tula said, tapping her chest. "Anyway. This is only a rank Orange location."

"What does that mean?" Daniel said with a frown.

"Mmm… well, you have mundane locations, non-ranked forests and the like. Those are where most villagers and Adventurers travel," Tula said, ticking her fingers off. "Doesn't mean there aren't monsters, but the monsters are rare and generally managed by sending Adventurers and guards.

"Then you have the Basic, Advanced and higher wilderness locations. We rank them the same way the Guild does, just to make it easier. But a Basic location is what you see in the deeper parts of unranked forests. The kind of dangers you'd expect to face normally."

"We once fought a Shadow Leopard," Daniel offered.

"Exactly. Like that. One kind of predator, nothing major. Advanced ranked areas see a wider range of monsters, with the highest threat predator marking the boundary of the danger," Tula said. "In this case, we're likely to see Orange class monsters at worse."

"So, why so many of us?" Daniel said, gesturing around at the large group.

"Because it's the wilderness," Tula said. "Go about another ten kilometers that way, we'll make it to the Esman Gorge. Where there's a rank Green-Blue threat. And just because they're ten kilometers away, it doesn't mean the raptors won't make their way here."

"Blue…" Daniel licked his lips.

"Green individually, blue in a group," Tula clarified. "The Nizhnye raptors are flying creatures of course, so they receive an increase in rank. They're semi-intelligent, with a low-level cunning that has them attacking only those who are injured or those they believe they can defeat. They also have a modicum of air elementalism, allowing them to form air armour and wind blades. The armour makes taking them with ranged weaponry difficult. Magic and powerful, singular attacks are the recommendations."

"Are you an encyclopedia or a person," Hjalmar said, the rogue somehow having managed to sneak up on the pair.

"This information is the minimum required of a Ranger to know," Tula said with a sniff. "I could also tell you about their mating habits and their preferred prey, but for an *Adventurer,* I think it's unnecessary."

As Hjalmar bristled, Daniel coughed into his hand before he took control of the conversation.

"What you're saying is that most expeditions are easy, until they're not?"

Tula sniffed at Daniel but had to reluctantly acknowledge his words. "There are worse things than an easy expedition."

"And now you've done it," Hjalmar said. "Idiot Ranger. Never say things could be worse. Never!" As the rogue stomped off to relay the idiocy of the Ranger to his friends, Daniel had to silently agree. Perhaps if he found some salt to throw over his shoulder…

Chapter 12

Ominous pronouncement or not, the expedition continued with their uneventful journey. Day in and day out, Daniel found himself either on the boats or, on rare occasion, working with the gatherers. As Craig realised Daniel's laughable level of accuracy with his crossbow, the Adventurer was never allowed to join the hunting party. The group had no use for an Adventurer who could not hit a barn door at fifty paces.

As the days continued, the campsite grew in size as tanning racks, curing and smoking stations were added. As each piece of hide, each morsel of meat was cured or smoked, Sava and the other merchants would store them away in their bags. Each bag was enchanted with dimensional storage attributes that doubled or tripled the volume within. After that, the merchant's individual Skills and Sava's expedition manager Skill then added to the storage amount. It was only because of the higher Levels of the merchants and Sava that this entire expedition would even make financial sense. Even so, by the time they hit the third week that they were in-forest, the merchants had begun to select and remove less expensive goods, setting them aside to be replaced with more commercially viable products.

Daniel yawned, working some leather oil into the greaves of his leather armour again. Mid-afternoon on a rest day meant Daniel was taking the time to care for his equipment. Hands moving in a small circular motion, he worked the oiled rag into the leather in parts, eyeing the scratches and discolorations. The armor was still in relatively good condition, though that could end at any time. But the motion of caring for it, of slowly massaging the armor in was meditative and restful.

"Incoming!"

Daniel jerked, dismissing the greaves as it nearly fell from his hands as the rag fluttered to the ground. Daniel grabbed for his hammer and shield, eyeing the direction the shout came from. A few seconds later, the harvesting team rushed in. Direction of threat confirmed, Daniel moved to take position in front of the entrance while other members of the rest team took their place too.

"Asin!" Daniel called once he was situated, shouting for his friend who was on guard again today.

"Orcs," Asin called. "Four... five?"

Daniel grunted, crouching down beneath his shield but forcing himself to relax tense muscles. No reason to stay tense, to use energy when the danger was not here yet. He would hear it when the rest came.

"What happened?" Daniel called out, hoping to get an answer. There was no reason for Orcs to be out here. They lived to the west on the plains mostly and rarely ventured into these forests.

"No idea. We were out gathering, and then boom, they shot Uwe. Omrak and Bjarne are holding them off, but we had to run," a familiar voice called back, the same one that first shouted a warning.

"Pack up!"

Daniel turned his head, spotting Sava running back in from the other entrance. As he turned, Daniel was surprised to see that the merchants were already packing up their bags, stuffing everything into their bags with practiced ease. "Get ready to move."

"Back, foul beasts! I am Omrak, son of Losin, an orange-ranked Advanced Adventurer and. You. Will. Not. Win!" Omrak roared, just before the telltale discharge of electricity from Omrak's skill exploded forth. The crackle and hiss of lightning, of leaves and branches hissing as they burnt, and the screams of strange monsters resounded.

"Come on, you blond oaf!" Bjarne cried.

In short order, the pair stumbled in, Omrak dragged backwards by Bjarne. As they stumbled into the clearing, enchanted globes were triggered by Vivian. The Sorcerer twisted her hands, setting the pre-prepared traps. A light yelp preceded a low yelp as a shadowed figure threw himself into a roll, just avoiding the newly set traps.

"Watch it, Viv!" Hjalmar snarled as he spun, his recurve bow appearing in his hand and an arrow nocking as he stared back the way he just came from.

"Sorry!" Vivian said, the mage's eyes tight.

Daniel ignored the commotion, having moved over to help Bjarne pull Omrak back and lay him down. Bjarne was feeding the Northerner a potion even as Daniel placed his hand over the man, eyeing the numerous cuts that criss-crossed the teenager's body. A particularly nasty cut had torn through the hardened, enchanted leather vest that Omrak wore, parting skin and muscle beneath and showing bone and portions of his innards.

Omrak, son of Losin (Level 16)
HP: 161/532 (Bleeding -8)

"Can you heal him?" Bjarne said.

"Yes," Daniel said. Already, he threw **Minor Healing II** on his friend, layering the spell again and again in short order, using a touch of his Gift to help stitch together the wounds that closed.

"Then I shall leave you," Bjarne said.

Daniel barely heard the words, his focus on his friend. The generic healing spell fixed everything, from the incipient bruises along the man's arms to the giant wound that pulsed blood, but with his hands pushing together flesh, Daniel was able to guide some of that healing. A flash of pain, a portion of his mind twisted away as he connected severed blood vessels. Then, the healing magic from the potion and his own spells washed over the wounds, stitching them together.

"Stay down. Let the spell fix you," Daniel ordered Omrak whose cloudy eyes were slowly clearing up. **"Healer's Mark."**

The time-delayed healing spell washed over Omrak, working to send pulses of healing energy into the Northerner.

"I can still fight…" Omrak said, his fist closing on his two-handed sword.

"Don't move, you idiot," Daniel said, shoving his friend down not too gently. Already, at the clearing, Daniel could the sounds of battle as sword met shield and ice-cold enchantments froze and slowed. "They have it. And I just healed you. If you pick up that sword again, you're just going to tear open your wounds."

Omrak growled but stayed lying down, though he squirmed around enough with pained grunts to roll his head around to watch the fight. Content that his friend was going to stay down, Daniel scooped up his hammer and stalked over to the entrance.

Hampered by the lamed bodies of their friends that had triggered the ice spike traps, the Orcs were having a hard time getting into the clearing. Bjarne stood at the forefront of the fight, stabbing and cutting with his halberd, the small shield strapped on his arm only occasionally used to block cuts that he could not react to in time with the haft of his polearm. By the side, Hjalmar had exchanged his bow for a pair of short swords that he used to defend and cut at arms and legs that approached too close. And behind them all, Vivian let loose bolts of fire while Asin sniped those at the back with the crossbow.

"On your left," Daniel called out to Bjarne as he took his place in the line. Together, the pair focused on holding the line. A quick block with his shield gave Daniel enough time to unleash a **Double Strike** that broke first an elbow then on the return swing lodge a spike in a thigh. Immediately, Daniel stepped back a little, giving his opponent time to stumble back as he bled his life away via a torn artery.

"We hold here," Daniel ordered the group. "And kill them slowly."

As if Daniel' words were an insult, the half-dozen remaining Orcs that still stood threw themselves at the Adventurers. After a half-dozen passes, Daniel's eyes tightened in surprise. He took another blow from a wildly swung mace, deflected it to the side, and gave the deflection a slight push to open the Orc further. A beat later, Daniel caught a sword strike on the haft of his axe, deflecting to the side with a slight spin before he used a reverse strike to sink the spike into the first Orc's shield. A pull brought the Orc stumbling forward and lowered the shield enough for Daniel's horizontally held shield rim to crush nose and cheekbones as the Adventurer triggered **Shield Bash.** Then, it was just a matter of blocking the next attack. The first few seconds of the holding action had the Orcs reeling, each contact with the Adventurer's enhanced, damaging aura

172

sending shocks through them. Even a blocked attack jarred, if not damaged.

The Orcs were strong and aggressive. Even with his own enhanced strength, Daniel found each blow hard to receive directly. But, strong or not, the creatures that used to be such dangerous threats were surprisingly easy. Their levels might be equal to his own Adventurer-ranked one, but they were specialized. And inexperienced. Unskilled. Raw and aggressive, but without the hint of polish that the Adventurers had. They did not even have a Soldier's discipline.

Perrin's Strike lashed out, coming in overhand with a short, sharp strike that crashed directly onto the remaining Orc's head. The blow crushed the head, pushing the creature's skull into its neck, blood splattering as light flashed around the hammer. A notification appeared—one that Daniel had not seen in ages.

Orc Warrior (Level 9) Summon Captured

Even as the monster staggered backwards, Hjalmar appeared behind it, sliding short swords into its torso and twisting. The monster kicked feebly before falling still, the rogue pushing the corpse aside. The three front line fighters panted, staring around the entrance to the clearing with wide eyes as they realised the fight was done.

"Orcs!" Another voice, this time from the other clearing.

Daniel jerked his head upwards, twisting to the other clearing. Already, he could see Elisa, Sumuhan, and Uppulu standing guard, the three having arrived back at some point in their fight. In moments, the last group of hunters arrived, stumbling in.

"Healer!" Voices rose, calling for Daniel.

"Go. We'll watch this clearing," Bjarne ordered.

Daniel hesitated, looking up to Asin who was stringing the crossbow. The Catkin was crouched forward, back leg claws extended and gripping the stone as her tail lashed out behind her. She caught Daniel's gaze, giving him a curt nod even as she watched for more trouble.

"Healing potion. Come on, come on!"

Daniel looked over to the injured merchants, the disemboweled man that was dying, his injuries too far gone for any simple potion. He bit his lips, but Daniel ran forwards to do his job. To heal while his friends killed.

***

"Knew this was a bad idea. Knew this was dumb. Stupid Ranger. Stupid Orcs," Asin growled under her breath in Catkin as she finished nocking the crossbow and placed it on her shoulder. The Catkin sighted down the weapon, exhaled, and then gently

pressed on the trigger. The knockback shook her shoulder briefly before the Catkin started nocking the crossbow again, her gaze still fixed on her target.

The crossbow bolt flew through the air, drawing a beautiful parabolic before it punched through thin leather armor and impaled the Orc Warrior. It staggered back, gurgling around its punctured lung and buying the fleeing Adventurers time. Craig and the remaining members of the hunting party were backing off, the hunting merchants aiding the group with a flurry of arrows. Asin growled softly, staring at the crossbow beneath her hands. Her Skill **Fan of Knives** or the aura from her bracer were useless at this range.

As she heaved, the Catkin turned her head sideways, thin but wiry muscles pulling as the string pulled back. Head turning sideways, Asin scanned for more trouble and found it. A loud yowl had the Adventurers look up at her.

"Patrol! Seven," Asin snarled out to the group, her finger pointing to where the orcs were approaching the first entrance. Damn it. They were going to be pinned in.

Standing up, the Beastkin's tail continued to lash out behind her as she scanned the forest, hoping to find clues of what else might be coming. But the dense foliage blocked the Beastkin's ability to see anything more, though instinct told her that the two groups coming forth were not the only one. There was no way that there were just a few patrols, not when there were so many. Though, it did raise the question of why and how there could be so many Orcs here. And, most importantly, as Asin scanned the campsite once again… Where was Tula?

***

Arrow Storm! The Skill triggered in silence, the Ranger hidden above in the foliage watching as her single arrow blossomed into a half-dozen more. They rained down on the Orc patrol from the Clay Spiders, landing amidst the hurrying group; killing one and injuring three others. Even as the group snarled and looked around for their attacker, the Ranger was backing off, disappearing into the woods again.

Four. The fourth patrol. Tula's lips curled up in a snarl even as she hurried away, pressing herself against a tree when the lumbering sounds of the Orc patrol that had been chasing her caught up. She slowed her breathing, stretching her senses to the maximum as she waited to see if she would be found out.

The Orcs lumbered past, missing the stealthy Ranger who continued to stay still, waiting. Her caution was soon proven vital as a last straggler came along, this one creeping by slowly. Tula waited, watching the monster walked past before she moved, nocking her arrow and triggering

---

Penetrating Strike. Even as the Orc flinched as the sound of the string loosening caught up to it, the arrow lodged itself in its throat and back of its neck, dropping the monster soundlessly.

Quickly, Tula hurried over to the body and pulled it aside, hiding the corpse in the undergrowth before patting it down. She tossed aside feather and stone fetishes after glancing at them briefly, pocketed the few coins the monster had and eyed the single, rotten piece of meat in its pouch.

Starving.

Tula shivered, her suspicions confirmed at last. The too thin Orcs, the unusual movements of the tribe, and their appearance in the Great Forest. This was a losing tribe. One driven from their home by a more powerful tribe. One that they had great enmity with, for otherwise, they would have just been subsumed. Now, they wandered, hoping to find a place to rest. Wandered and starved.

Body covered, the Ranger stood up and debated her next course of action. By the time she had learnt of their movements, the fast-moving Orc patrols had encountered the first hunting party. Once that happened, an encounter was guaranteed. Bad luck that she had been checking the traps on the other side of the perimeter when they had entered.

Now, the only question was how to reduce the damage. Tula stood silently, considering and discarding plans in quick order. The Orcs would go after the hunters and find the campsite. That much was guaranteed. They would know that any expedition would have food—more than they currently had. So the group's best option was to run. Tula made a face, looking to where the campsite was.

However, the majority of the Orc patrols were between her and the encampment. It was going to take time for her to make her way back. And it would be nearly impossible to sneak into the camp itself. In that case, she could only hope that the Catkin's secondary escape plan worked.

Chapter 13

Daniel finished bandaging the wound around the merchant's leg and then looked around for water. Finding the bucket another merchant had dropped by him, he dunked his hands in it, washing the blood off before shaking the excess water away. The smell of blood and vomit mixed with the burnt flesh and wood smell of fires ahead, reminding Daniel of the fight that still rung through the clearing. Hands dry, Daniel was turning to the next patient.

Instead of another injured merchant, Craig dropped down beside Daniel, cradling one gashed forearm. Without thinking, Daniel eyed the wound and splashed water over it, washing out the bleeding wound to eye the damage. No foreign matter, no leather stuck in it. The bandage Daniel grabbed went around the limb, wrapping around it again and again as he began the spell formulation in his mind.

"How goes it?" Daniel asked, looking up to the clearing gaps. The merchant fighters had picked up their spears, joining the fight at a distance to help the undermanned Adventurers to hold off the Orcs. Twenty minutes into the fight, Daniel had yet to move from the improvised aid station they had set-up for him.

"We hold," Craig said. "**Healer's Mark** is sufficient. I have a regenerative Skill."

Daniel paused before he nodded, finishing the incantation. His hands, in the midst of wrapping the bandage, paused as they glowed and layered the spell on the man before Daniel finished tying off the bandage. "You're good."

"I'll send the next back," Craig said.

Daniel could only nod dumbly, eyeing his Mana as Craig trotted back to the front lines. Even if the man was acting nonchalant, Daniel recalled hearing the harsh breathing, and he sensed the heightened heartbeat and buildup of lactic acid in the man's muscles. It was hard to hide things from a Healer, especially one that had just finished casting a spell of healing on you.

As Sumuhan jogged over, Daniel dismissed the thoughts from his mind as he checked on his Mana. After a couple of casts of **Minor Healing II** when an Adventurer or Merchant had been damaged too greatly and repeated casts of **Healer's Mark**, he was running low. Now, Daniel really ached to have an upgrade of his healing spells. If he had known he would be stuck playing healer…

Mana: 157/252

"How many healing potions do we have left?" Daniel asked his helper. The man looked down at the small pile of potions in their container, counting them over before replying.

"Six high, four middle, and eight low grade, Healer."

"Not a Healer," Daniel corrected. "But thank you." Of course, Daniel knew that number did not include the individual potions some of the Adventurers carried. These were just the expedition's potions—the ones that had been purchased for emergencies. Since high and middle-end potions could last for years, the purchase of them could be considered an investment. As for low-end potions, they could easily be resold if necessary. Smart expedition managers – like Sava – ensured they had more than enough on hand, for most situations.

Most, not including a full-frontal assault by a clan of Orcs.

And then, there was no more time as Hjalmar appeared beside Daniel, limping and favoring his leg.

***

An hour later, Daniel threw one last strike with his hammer at an Orc, making sure it backed off properly before he stepped back too, lowering his hammer. The Orcs backed off, disappearing into the cover of foliage and behind their shields as they rested and waited for more reinforcements. In turn, the Adventurers and fighting Merchants took a break, drinking water and bandaging wounds. Letting his hammer fall by its wrist strap, Daniel turned to look at his compatriots, checking for damage and for what he could do. Surprisingly, no shouts of 'healer' erupted, relieving Daniel. He still had a few spells left, but his slowly regenerating Mana was best used for utter emergencies.

"How many?" Daniel asked Sava as he came by, offering a waterskin. As Sava answered, Daniel washed his face with a handful of water before consuming a good quarter of the bottle. Fighting was hard and thirsty work.

"Asin said there were at least two more patrols that joined. So, thirty? Forty?" Sava said.

"They have brought their Orc Raiders and higher leveled Warriors," Omrak rumbled. Having allowed himself to heal, the big Northerner had taken his place in the front line with Daniel, the pair of Adventurers making a formidable force after so much time working together. Backed up with a few merchants with their spears and Rob with his spells, the group had held one clearing entirely by themselves while Craig's team had taken the other side, healing and resting in the meantime. "The battles have been getting harder."

"True," Daniel said, brow furrowing. The silent entrance to the clearing seemed to grow ever more ominous as Daniel stared at it, his breath shorting as he considered their future. Healing potions had decreased, Mana had faded, and even Asin's bolts from above had stopped falling as often. Even now, the non-combatant merchants were pulling out arrows and bolts from corpses, shoving the bodies about to create a blockade. Daniel knew they would bring those arrows and bolts back to the archers, but many were unrecoverable.

"Can we hold?" Sava asked softly, dropping his voice as he stepped close to Daniel.

Daniel glanced to the side, seeing how some of the merchants had stopped their actions to listen in to his answer. Daniel hesitated for a second before he answered, "Yes." But that hesitation was telling. One that made Sava tighten his lips in dissatisfaction. "We should speak with Craig."

Sava nodded, and Daniel waved to the resting Adventurers to make sure they knew to take his place. Once he was certain that the clearing would hold, Daniel led Sava over to the other Adventuring captain, the trio meeting in a clearing midway between both entrances.

"What?" Craig said.

"The Orcs keep getting reinforcements," Daniel said.

"I know. We've killed at least twenty of their men," Craig said. He pressed his lips together as he regarded the narrow entrances to the clearing and then the broken-down masonry clogged with vegetation that made up the rest. "It might be harder to get in outside the clearing, but at some point, even Orcs will try it. At that time…"

"We cannot hold," Sava said.

"I would not say cannot," Craig rebutted.

"But it'd be hard," Daniel said, shaking his head. "We'd need to keep those on rest right now on alert. We'd be expanding our front further."

"Then, what, we breakthrough?" Craig said, looking at the clearing. "Even if we managed to do that, we'd be forced to fight in the forest. And where would we go?"

"Way out. Up there," Asin said, interrupting the group. The Catkin offered a toothy smile while pointing to her guard post. The group frowned, staring up at the steep climb off the ruins.

"Then what? We'd still be in the forest," Craig said with a snort.

"No," Asin said. She chopped her hand down firmly. "Cliff. Forest. Gorge."

"The Esman Gorge?" Sava said and Asin nodded. "That… I was willing to risk it earlier, but with the Orcs, they would stir up the raptors for sure."

"Yes. Distraction," Asin nodded quickly.

"I don't know. The Ranger…"

"Talked. Agreed," Asin said, flashing a wide smile at Sava. "Backup."

"Yes, the Ranger who is not here now. Who we need to make our way through the gorge safely," Craig said, his fist clenching tightly in frustration.

"Tula will find us," Daniel assured Craig. He looked over to Asin, the Catkin flashing Daniel a confident smile before he drew a deep breath. "Look. Our chances of surviving are low, especially if there are more Orcs coming. I don't know how many there are, but them pulling back like this makes me think there's more. And probably higher Level leaders. If we can avoid a fight…"

Craig tapped his foot, looking back and forth between the clearings and the ruins, hesitation clear on his face.

"I'll trust the Ranger, if I have a say in this," Sava said. Now that a fight had begun, the actual command of the expedition had devolved to the Ranger and the Adventurers. Without Tula, it was Craig in charge.

"Trust her…" Craig said, then sighed in defeat. "Fine. If we die, I'm going to bitch at you all down the river."

"Done," Daniel said. "So, what now?"

Craig frowned, his mind obviously spinning through options. In short order, he began giving out orders to Sava and Daniel. Asin was called upon to provide even more information, which resulted in Sumuhan coming over to translate and expand upon the concepts from the Catkin. And all the while, Daniel could not help but glance back towards the clearing, wondering when the next attack would arrive. And if they would make it in time.

***

"Up!" Asin said, calling down to the Merchants. Holding onto their bags, the group had ascended the ruins, dragging their tired bodies and their luggage up. Perched next to Asin, Elisa helped the Merchants up, offering a hand and directing them to the top of the ridge where a pair of ropes hung, waiting for them.

"Here they come," Elisa said, moving away from the Merchants to clear her line of fire. "I got two."

"Omrak, remember to pull back when we tell you to," Daniel warned his big friend. The Northerner sniffed in reply, the tip of his sword resting on the ground as he conserved energy. Daniel shot a worried look at his silent friend before he dismissed the concerns. It was nothing he could do about it, not right now. "Rob, are you ready?"

"Spheres are ready. After this, I'll be down to only two charged spheres," Rob said. "I hate leaving them here…"

"Better your spheres than our necks."

"True enough," Rob said. "What are they doing over that side?"

Daniel shrugged, unsure how the other team intended to break contact. He had just been assured that they had their ways.

When the Orcs made their way to the entrance, they were not charging but moving in a slow, steady and guarded formation. Like the previous patrols, the Orcs were wielding an assortment of weapons ranging from clubs to swords and shields. Surprisingly, few of the Orcs carried spears, bows or crossbows. When they reached the clearing, they stared at the group, letting out low snarls. As a crossbow bolt lodged in the chest bone of one of the few unshielded Orcs in the front line, they howled and threw themselves forwards as if the attack was a signal.

Daniel braced himself, judging the fast-closing distance before stepping forwards as they were nearing and triggering his **Shield Bash** ability. The attack smashed into a charging Orc's shield and rebounded, throwing Daniel back as the combined effects of the monster's **Bloodrush Charge** and **Shield Bash** overwhelmed him. As he scrambled to keep his footing, the next Orc was on him, lashing out with a spiked club that Daniel barely managed to block. Before it could continue its attack, Omrak stepped forward and brought his sword down in a double-handed overhand blow that split apart the hide helm and stuck halfway through the monster's skull. Omrak reacted immediately, stepping forwards and kicking the dying Orc back, shoving it away from him.

As another Orc moved forwards to take the dead Orc's place, Daniel finally recovered his footing and timing, blocking a strike and returning one against his original opponent. He kept his shield up, making sure to guard against attacks and only lashing out occasionally. Like Omrak beside him, the pair fought carefully, more intent on taking sure shots rather while keeping themselves safe rather than killing their opponents. In short order, the Orcs realised the difference and started to push forwards aggressively.

Rob, standing behind, raised his hands and released a **Magic Arrow**, the Mana-formed attack cutting through armor and injuring an Orc as it stepped forward. Taking advantage of the situation, Daniel hunched down and shattered the monster's knee as the Orc reeled, forcing it to fall backwards and clogging up the entrance again.

Seconds turned into minutes as the pair of Adventurers continued to fight carefully. Even when the Orcs finally managed to pull their injured comrades out, the pair did not push forwards, content to injure and slow their opponents. And through it all, Daniel listened with half an ear out.

"Northeast!" Sava cried out in warning.

Daniel growled, unable to look away but knowing that the Orcs must be attempting to breach the circle in another way. It was one of the reasons they added Elisa to the guard post, giving the group another ranged attacker. As he blocked another attack, an enchanted spike popped up above his shoulder and swooped in to blind the Orc. The monster stumbled back, clutching its damaged eye.

"What is taking them so long?" Omrak panted, a new cut along an arm bleeding freely and forming a sticky mess beneath his fingers. Daniel eyed his friend, concern about the continuing loss of blood but unable to do anything about it right this moment. Surrounding the Northerner, a low red glow filled the man, a mark of the growing Rage ability.

"Should be soon…" Daniel said.

"Southeast!" Sava shouted.

"Damn it…" Rob cursed behind.

But Daniel and Omrak no longer had time to talk, as the Orcs threw themselves at the pair with renewed fury. Once again, they fought, careful not to trigger any of their stamina-draining Skills. They just had to hold. Hold…

"CLEAR!" Sava cried.

Immediately, Daniel triggered **Perrin's Blow**, the strike coming in at an angle that caught his opponent on the weapon, sending it bouncing off the monster's own chest. Forced to take a step back to absorb the impact, the Orc had to further edge backwards and duck as Omrak threw a wide overhand cut with his giant sword.

Disengaged, Daniel moved back as Rob clapped his hands together. From beneath the churned earth, buried enchanted orbs exploded, a cloud of poisonous gas flowing up. Daniel and Omrak both retreated immediately, the greenish-purple gas continuing to boil out of the spheres.

Surprisingly, the clouds did not move much from their original location, instead staying concentrated as they continued to rise.

"Let's go. It will only hold for a few minutes," Rob said. Behind the cloud of smoke, the Orcs watched, staring as the Adventurers fell back. A glance over to the other entrance showed the entrance covered in sticky webs, one of which had the weakly thrashing body of an Orc captured within. As the Adventurers turned and ran towards the crumbled ruins, the Orcs let out a howl of anger.

As a group, the Adventurers reached the bottom of the crumbled stones where the Merchants stood at the top, only a few of them still waiting to make their way down. Sava who had called the 'Clear' was halfway up the ruins already when Daniel reached the bottom. The healer turned around, setting himself as he got ready to take the back. As Omrak came to a halt, Daniel snarled.

"Go!"

"I shall…"

"We need a fighter at the other end. Go!" Daniel snapped.

Omrak hesitated for a second more before he nodded and started scrambling up after the Selkie who had never even stopped. Daniel smiled briefly while the other group of Adventurers managed to make their way over, the squishy casters making their way first while Craig and the melee fighters waited for their turn.

"You should go," Craig said to Daniel.

"I've got a shield…"

"And you're the healer," Craig said flatly. Daniel hesitated but grimaced, pausing only long enough to slap his hand and a spell on the injured Bjarne before he turned around to wait his turn. Finding himself standing beside Hjalmar, he eyed the Rogue.

"I'm fine. Nothing my healing potions couldn't fix," Hjalmar said.

Before Daniel could reply, a shout from the Orcs drew his attention back. Rather than wait for the cloud to disperse, the monsters had thrown themselves through it, picking up the poison as they charged the group. On the other side, the sticky magical webbing had been set on fire, the body of the captured Orc twitching feebly.

"Shit. They're berserk!" Craig said. "Elisa, Vivian!"

In answer, magic and mundane arrows fell, harrying the rushing monsters. Hjalmar slapped Daniel's shoulder, jerking his head to the broken rubble before he started scrambling up. Daniel sighed and took off, ascending quickly. As he reached the top, he looked back down to see both Craig and Uppulu caught in battle, the two Adventurers fighting to keep the swarming Orcs back.

"We need to clear some space," Hjalmar said. He held his hand out, pulling his quiver and bow from his inventory before firing down at the group.

"Daniel!" Asin snorted, making the Adventurer look over. He turned and caught the crossbow that had been tossed to him and then the nearly empty quiver. Even as he watched, Asin reached for her knives and bunched her feet beneath herself.

"Asiiiin!" Daniel cried out, too late as the Catkin threw herself off the rocks. The Catkin fell, knives held in hand and landed right on top of a pair of Orcs, slamming both to the ground as her knives bore into their body. The Catkin, like her namesake, bounced right back up unlike her victims, pulling new knives from her sheaths as she cut into hamstrings of surprised monsters.

"**Flame Serpent!**" Vivian cried out. From her hand, a living snake of flame and smoke formed and flew down, ducking and dancing through the group. The Sorcerer staggered, her face as white as the petal of a baby breath flower as she drained her Mana in that attack. Combined with Asin's distraction, the two Adventurers managed to end their attackers and swiftly begin climbing while Asin disengaged by tossing a **Fan of Knives** and then bounding up the rocks.

As the fastest recovering Orc started climbing up, Daniel finally nocked and fired his crossbow. The bolt arced down and missed its intended target, shattering the rock just in front of the monster. The explosive destruction made the Orc flinch backwards, a shard cutting an eye open and making the monster fall backwards. Rob, standing at the top waved his hands around, sending his enchanted spikes to harry the Orcs as well as they attempted to climb up.

"I'm out!" Elisa said as she stored her bow.

"Go!" Daniel ordered the woman. Daniel looked over at Vivian who continued to look pale, then pointed at her to Bjarne as he managed to make his way up. "Get her down."

Directing the group as he readied his own last bolt, Daniel stared down at the group of Orcs and thanked the stars that they continued to be bereft of ranged weaponry. Even with the harrying attacks of Asin, himself and Hjalmar, the Orcs continued to make their way up, a short ten feet beneath the others.

"Go!" Daniel said when Craig and Uppulu made it up to his level.

"I should stay…" Craig protested.

"I've got a plan. Now, go!" Daniel snapped. A flash of loss ran through Daniel as he stared at the ropes. Once, a long time ago, he knew how to rappel, how to tie off knots and move with surety. But that time had gone, taken away by his Gift. Broken memories resided within him, portions of memories taken not just from his mind but his body. But, still, he knew in theory how to rappel down.

Craig hesitated a moment longer before taking off down the ropes, allowing the healer to fire his last bolt at the leading Orc and, finally, managing to land a shot. The impact of the bolt threw the monster back, sending it tumbling down off the hill and making Daniel grin savagely. By this time, Asin hopped up beside him, triggering one last **Fan of Knives** before she paused, panting.

"Get down," Daniel ordered.

The Catkin did not even hesitate, gripping the nearest rope and climbing down with ease. In short order, the Beastkin was sliding down the rope, leaving Daniel alone on the top of the ruin. As the Orcs continued to clamber up, he grinned and released his last present.

The summoned Orc Warrior that appeared beside him glared at Daniel for a second before turning around and squatting, waiting for its living brethren to make their way forwards. While the Orcs were distracted by the summoning, Daniel checked and then cut the first empty rope before grabbing the second. Setting his feet against the rock wall, Daniel threw himself down the line, gripping and releasing the rope at intervals as he fell down the cliff. At the last few feet, his momentum grew too much and he found his fingers losing their grip and he landed awkwardly on his back, his breath driven from him. The Adventurer groaned, thankful that he had managed to avoid a concussion. Even as he lay on the ground, recovering his breath, Rob waved his hand. An enchanted, magical spike shifted, slicing the rope apart near the top and sending the now loose end dropping to land on the feet of the surprised Adventurer.

"What the hell?"

"No time," Rob said, pointing upwards to allow Daniel to see the glowering faces of the Orcs that had managed to kill his summon. "Come on. Time to go."

Daniel groaned, taking a proffered arm from Asin as he staggered upwards. He focused, sending a wash of healing magic through himself and clearing some of the bruises before he stored the rope in his inventory. With the easy access down cut-off, the Orcs could only glower at the Adventurers as they took off. So far, so good.

Chapter 14

Daniel quickly joined the main section of the group, moving up the line as he eyed the team with a practiced eye. The healer checked for injuries, layering a **Healer's Mark** twice on those who most needed the spell, allowing the healing spell time to do its work. It was not as effective as the group was moving, but it was better than nothing.

"The ropes are cut?" Craig said when Daniel made his way nearly up to the front.

"Yes," Daniel said. "Who's leading us?"

"The Catkin and Sava both have an idea of where we need to go," Craig said. "I have Hjalmar and Sumuhan at the rear, with your friend Omrak backing them up."

Daniel nodded, lips pressed tight as he checked over the group. Because only a quarter of the merchants had been part of the fighting, the non-combatants were mostly in good shape. However, the fighters were all injured, many of them bearing hastily wrapped bandages and half-healed wounds. With barely fifty Mana left, Daniel knew he had to make sure to let his Mana regenerate, no matter how much he would want to fix their injuries.

"How long do you think we have?" Daniel finally asked.

Craig shrugged before he said, "That's more a question for our non-present Ranger. Just run. Our lead will not be that long."

Daniel nodded and fell silent, conserving his oxygen as he ran alongside.

Over an hour passed with no sign of pursuit, a surprising fact that made Daniel even more worried. They jogged, pausing every twenty minutes to slow down and rest. From his understanding, they had four hours before they reached the gorge. And, while Daniel dreaded the pursuit, he knew they needed it too.

"Faster," Tula said, appearing from the undergrowth. Craig, who had been running alongside Daniel, jerked as the Ranger made her presence known.

"Where have you been?" Craig questioned the Ranger.

"Dealing with patrols and scouting," Tula said. She ducked her head slightly, hiding her eyes for a brief moment before she added. "It's good you escaped. But there's a whole displaced clan coming."

"Damn it," Craig snarled. "I knew it."

"They're at the camp, taking what food they can and feeding their people. They were starving," Tula said. "It's good that you left some of the food for them. It should give us some time."

"Didn't do it on purpose," Sava said grumpily.

"I know. But it still works," Tula said.

"Why are they in such a state?" Daniel said. "Shouldn't they have hunters?"

"Many probably died when they were driven out," Tula said. "The few they do have won't be enough to feed the remaining tribe."

"Ranger, what is the plan?" Sava said. "Do we still go to the gorge?"

"Yes," Tula said with a nod. "I'll lead us in. Follow my directions. We'll be entering the gorge and sneaking our way through it as the best option. If all goes well, the raptors will be drawn to the Orcs as they follow us."

"And if doesn't?" Craig said suspiciously.

"Then I have a backup plan too," Tula said. "But we must move."

Under the suspicious gaze of Craig and Sava, Tula headed to the front of the group, taking over leading the group. Almost immediately, they shifted directions slightly as the well-travelled Ranger took over.

***

Another two hours went by, Daniel's Mana slowly inching upwards. He eyed the third more that had increased in the time, debating if he should use some of it now or wait. Healing some of his companions would help speed up their escape, but it would reduce the amount of Mana he had if things went south. After briefly weighing the risks, Daniel decided to hold onto his Mana for now. Later, perhaps.

As he pushed his thoughts away, voices from behind him made Daniel turn. He frowned, realising that the muttering was coming from the rearguard. He slowed slightly, before remembering that he needed to keep to his position. His job was to keep an eye out for trouble coming in from the sides. Even if there was an attack, without a call for help, he should stay in position. After all, it could be a feint.

In short order, the noise of battle from behind fell away. Daniel turned his head, eyeing the guards who ran behind, many who were doing the same. There was no signal, no indication that there was anything further to be concerned about, and so, head down, Daniel continued to run. Thankfully for his fraying nerves, word soon came up via a Merchant denoted as a runner. The rearguard had clashed with Orc Scouts and had missed at least one. Potentially more, if the Scouts had stacked themselves in their search. In either case, they had been found.

The news was a shot of adrenaline that promulgated through the entire group, sending a burst of energy that resulted in a faster pace. Unfortunately, the faster pace could not be held for long, and the group started to slow, the marathon session taking its toll on the Merchants and Adventurers. Omrak reached into a belt-pouch, extracting an orange-colored flask from which he sipped on. Seeing the questioning glances shot his way, Omrak spoke.

"Stamina potion," Omrak said. His words engendered a series of requests from the Merchants. The Northerner was obviously reluctant, but finally, he offered a few sips to those about. As he carefully watched his precious potion being passed around, Omrak said to Daniel. "I am surprised Sava has no such potions."

"He had a few. But Sava was using low-grade healing potions in their stead," Daniel said. He could understand the reasoning. A low-grade healing potion was not much more expensive than a dedicated Stamina potion, and both were, in the end, similar in their effects. While he had no understanding of how they were made, Daniel knew that Stamina potions basically provided a boost in nutrients and sped-up an individual's metabolism, particularly around muscles, hearts, and the lungs of imbibers. Healing potions did much the same, but with a focus on blood flow and production of the healing chemicals and cells. It still meant that individuals felt better and gained in their stamina as a side effect, just not as effectively. For a Merchant though who only needed marginal improvements most likely, it was just as good.

"And now we must save them for… SNAKE!" Omrak called out in warning, causing a number of the Merchants to stumble. Before anyone else could locate the monster, the Northerner had lobbed his throwing axe at the creature that was in the midst of dropping onto an unsuspecting Merchant, catching it on its body and tearing it away from its wooden perch. As the injured monster dropped, Omrak drew his double-handed large sword and began to chop it apart, never allowing the monster to regain the momentum in the fight. Even as it emitted a freezing chill through the surroundings, the Northerner never let up, only hopping back when the monster was in multiple parts. Daniel slowed down slightly before he assured himself that his friend had the matter well in-hand and sped up to retake his post.

"Good job," Craig said from behind to Omrak. "Now, get moving."

Head turning, Daniel kept looking for trouble. Sooner or later, the Orcs or more monsters would turn up.

***

The cliff faces of the gorge began to loom up before the group as they ran, the once magnificent river having shrunk in size leaving an undergrowth-strewn passage. On the bare cliff faces, stubborn trees and shrubs grew on any available space, only pushed aside by the brown nests of the raptors. In the very centre of the gorge, a small river trickled along, carrying the latest rainfall away.

As the group closed in on the gorge, Tula gathered everyone around and started handing out small pouches. From the pouches, a rancid, decomposing odour emitted, one so powerful that it choked the recipients even as the drawstrings of the pouches were drawn close.

"What is that?"

"Copper King Monkey feces," Tula said. Daniel gulped, dread filling his stomach when Tula mentioned the contents. He had an inkling of what this could be, but he was desperate for his guess to be wrong. Sadly, his expectations were to bear fruit and his hopes crushed. "Rub this on your clothing. Not your skin! The fermented feces will irritate your skin if."

"What? No!" Hjalmar protested.

"The Copper King Monkeys travel through the gorge in packs, stealing and feeding on the Nizhnye raptor's eggs and chicks. On scenting the monkeys, the Nizhnye will move aside. But because the raptors have a low sense of smell, the fermented feces is a must," Tula said. "Now quickly. Before the Orcs find us."

To the mass grumbling of the group, drawstrings were pulled apart and their malodorous contents applied over clothing and shoes.

"These are enchanted robes. My best pair too…" Rob said, even as he spread the feces over the formerly dark-blue material. "I'll have to pay extra to have this cleaned."

"Just be glad you have an Inventory to store it away in later," a nearby Merchant said. "I'm just going to toss mine."

"Less whining, more spreading," Daniel ordered the pair.

"You don't seem to be as affected," Vivian said, her face scrunched up as she dipped another finger into the pouch and carefully added the contents to her clothing. "You're nearly as unbothered as the Ranger."

"I'm a healer. This is not the worst thing I've dealt with," Daniel said. In particular, being a healer in an Adventuring town was the worse. Flesh that continued to slowly rot and dissolve because of a curse, and torn open abdomens which pulsed and writhed as parasites from the seventh Level ate and grew within. No. Fermented feces was the least of the things he had dealt with.

Once the group was ready, Tula brought them forwards at a much slower pace, the Ranger occasionally eyeing the sky. Bunched up together, the entire group focused on moving forwards into the dangerous gorge and, hopefully, allowing their pursuers to take the attacks of the inhabitants.

***

The gorge, on closer inspection, was a mixture of brown, orange and grey walls mixed with vivid greens of the flora and the occasional – and dangerous – splash of colour. After so many weeks in the Great Forest, Daniel knew that most plants that were vividly coloured were poisonous or just attempting to attract a monster. Only a very small number were not dangerous, using the camouflage of the dangerous flora to survive.

The group snuck closer, moving through the undergrowth and attempting to avoid the keen eyesight of the raptors. Of course, it was mostly a failure, since most of the creatures could easily pick the cultivators out. Even at a glance, Daniel could see how many of the raptors were watching them as they moved along on the floor. Yet, somehow, they chose not to attack.

As the group finally entered the gorge, first one, then a flock of the raptors took to wing. Without requiring a signal, the group froze, crouching lower as the expedition members awaited the attack. But, to their surprise, the raptors instead flew away, heading past the group.

Only when the last of the raptors had passed over them did the expedition begin moving. Yet, curiosity kept driving Daniel to look behind, curious to see why and where the flock of raptors had gone. In short order, the group of raptors began to dive, their target hidden in the foliage.

"What…?" Daniel muttered. Could it be the Orcs? If so, they were a lot closer than he had expected.

For a time, Daniel watched the birds fly in and out as they snuck deeper into the gorge, catching glimpses of the swooping avians before they were blocked by foliage and the curve of the land again.

"Are they still in the same place?" Daniel said to Elisa who was squatting on the slope a little farther up from him, watching the commotion behind them.

"Looks to be it. But there are fewer raptors… Ah!" Elisa said and breathed the last word out.

"What?" Daniel said, craning his neck back.

"The raptors have left."

"Damn." Daniel pressed his lips together in thought but then sighed. It seemed that relying on the raptors—at least this flock—to keep the Orcs back would be futile. "Do you think they'll still keep coming?"

"Why not?" Elisa said. "Nizhnye raptors might not taste that good, but if you're starving, it's good eating."

"You sound… experienced," Daniel said.

"Monster meat is quite edible, even if it does taste strange at times," Elisa said. "My parents were Questors, so I followed them on their missions as we grew up. A lot of time, the only thing we had to eat was monster meat."

"Huh," Daniel said, looking at Elisa with renewed interest. Adventuring families were not uncommon—just like some people might grow up to be Healers or Merchants or Farmers because of their family background, some Adventurers grew into the profession because of their parents. They were more uncommon, of course, the sheer number of deaths from Adventuring put a damper on long dynasties. But, in general, Adventuring families were better trained and better equipped to start with, reducing their losses.

"Surprised?" Elisa said.

"No. Well, sort of?" Daniel shrugged. "Never really thought about it. Must be nice, having Adventuring parents."

"There are good points. They're very proud I'm already Advanced," Elisa said, then she narrowed her eyes at the still Adventurer. "And they would really like it if I made it home. So get moving."

Daniel ducked his head in acknowledgement before he went and rejoined the Merchants. If he recalled the map, the gorge ran for miles before they exited the gap between the mountains and it became much wider. In the widened gorge, there were a number of exits that they could use to return to the village. Of course, to get there, they would need quite a few hours.

***

A hand came up and the group slowed as they moved to hide themselves beneath a hand overhang. The expedition members flopped down against the cliff walls while a few Adventurers took station around the perimeter. As Daniel jogged in among the group, he could not help but exhale in gratitude as his weak legs finally stopped moving.

"Eat. Refill water bottles. Rest for half-hour," Tula said.

Sava made a face as he walked over to the Ranger, dropping his voice as he spoke. "You are pushing us too hard."

"One hour left," Tula said. "We are not safe so long as we stay in the gorge."

"Why?" Daniel asked, letting his gaze fall on the opposite cliff face. "Your… solution for the raptors worked."

"There's something else," Tula said, touching a piece of dried feces on her clothes. "The monkeys would keep the raptor numbers in check normally, but they are none present at all. Something else must have driven them away."

"Oh…" Daniel said, rubbing his temples. Of course, there was something else. And with their luck, they were bound to encounter it. That's just the way it worked. Never simple. Daniel drew a deep breath, then slowly let it out, eyeing his mostly recovered Mana. Best to get fixing everyone else then.

After rest, food, and a reapplication of the feces, the group stood as they got ready to begin the last portion of their journey. As Daniel checked his armor and weapons, he let his gaze run over his weary, road-worn companions. Even the hardy Omrak and Uppulu were looking tired, their weapons drooping in their hands. Asin flashed Daniel a weary smile, her fur matted with sweat and other unmentionables as she crouched in one corner, watching. And Tula, the Ranger, was perhaps the most exhausted of them all. Frowning, Daniel walked over to Tula and reached out to grab her hand.

"What?" Tula said, flushing as Daniel raised her hand and took it in both of his.

"Spell," Daniel said. The Healer focused deep within, pulling on his Gift and sending it through her. First was the blood, a simple cleansing and refreshing to give her more oxygen and removing the majority of the impurity buildups. Then, her muscles, following the flow of blood to touch upon the lactic acid buildup in her muscles, washing away a portion of it. It was a similar action to what he did for himself and his team before, a simple cleansing that kept them in tiptop condition in the Dungeons.

And with it, he felt another memory, another piece of himself slide away. Nothing much, a few seconds, a few minutes. Nothing at all… Unless it was a hug, a smile, a lesson.

Tula shuddered before she straightened unconsciously, eyes narrowing as she looked at Daniel. "What was that?"

"Spell," Daniel said and then released her hand. And no matter how suspiciously the Ranger looked at Daniel, he refused to elaborate.

"If you two are done, we should get moving," Craig said. "You can play lovebirds later."

Daniel snorted at Craig's words while Tula flushed again. But she waved the group on more energetically, her body refreshed. Yet, the hints of exhaustion could still be seen, if you knew where to look. Daniel could heal her body, but her mind was another thing.

Chapter 15

A short couple of miles from their turnoff, a silence extended across the Esman Gorge such that even the low-level chitter of animals and the occasional cry of the raptors had disappeared. Except for the rustle of wind in the day, an unnatural silence permeated the forest.

"What is it?" Daniel muttered to himself softly, but no one had an answer for him. The group instinctively gathered together, Elisa and Asin both moving up the slope to get a better view while the mages gathered their spells for quick dispersal. Tula turned her head from side to side, searching for the problem, for the cause until a finger rose from one of the Merchants.

"There!" he cried.

All eyes shifted, taking in the new sight and more than one jaw dropped as they realised what they were seeing. At first, it was just a single bird, brown and white against the cloudy grey-white skies that threatened rain. But then, other, smaller shadows in the sky resolved, shadows that were twice, three times as small.

"A mutated Nizhnye raptor," Tula breathed. "That's what happened to the monkeys."

Daniel knew of these mutants. Creatures that underwent evolution due to the consumption of other monsters or an encounter with some supernatural opportunity or disaster. The mutation was never controlled and could just as easily kill or injure the mutant monsters. But, if a mutant survived, it was often bigger, stronger and more dangerous than its un-mutated brethren. It was not uncommon for mutants to increase in threat level by two, three levels, sometimes more.

"Everyone! Wash the feces off. Quickly!" Tula said, the Ranger already suiting actions to words. There was a hesitation in the group, the order all too sudden.

"The mutant is what drove the monkeys away. It's hunting them!" Tula said, washing and splashing her fingers across dirty armor. "Damn it. We need Cleansing spells."

"Will this work?" Craig asked, the older Adventurer with a flask of alcoholic wine in his hand that he used to wash himself rather than water. It was a strange choice in Daniel's view, but he ignored it as he hastily washed himself clean.

"A bit," Tula said. "If we replace the scent with ours…"

"Can we not beat it?" Omrak rumbled, the big Adventurer eyeing the fast-approaching raptor and the flock that flew with it. "There are so many of us."

"It's not a question of if we can beat it," Craig said in reply. "But more about the Orcs that are coming behind."

"How close are they?" Daniel said, turning his gaze to their back trail. To keep their people together, they had withdrawn their rearguard so that there was no good way to tell how far back the Orcs were. Oh, there were a couple of occasions when a flock of raptors had been disturbed and launched themselves at the Orcs, but it seemed that even the raptors could learn. The last attack had been an hour ago, and at that time, the Orcs were an estimated mile behind.

"Who knows? But we'll have to guess it's close," Craig said.

Daniel nodded, drawing a deep breath before finishing his wash. Tula quickly waved the group to move on ahead, having given directions to Sumuhan and Bjarne who were leading the column in the front while she extracted a series of all too familiar pouches from her storage location.

"What are you doing?" Daniel said.

"Setting up a distraction," Tula said. "Go. I'll catch up."

Daniel hesitated but the Ranger shook her head, waving him on. Reluctantly, Daniel took off, knowing that he could do little to help her. This, the wilderness, was more her place than his. Still, he could only hope that what she planned was sufficient. And if not. Well. They'd work out later.

***

The group had made it only a few hundred meters before Tula appeared next to the group, running beside them as the group hurried forwards. Behind, the heavy flap of wings broke out behind them, the screech of the enormous mutant raptor sounding out behind. The group flinched at the screech, instinctively crouching lower as they ran.

A couple of the Merchants froze up, only to be grabbed by the hardy Adventurers who dragged them forwards.

"What did you do?" Daniel said as he dropped back a little to speak with Tula.

"Set up bait," Tula said, looking back. "The raptors will be there for a bit, eating."

Daniel nodded, grateful that at least that seemed to be working. Rather than continue talking, the pair ran, Tula occasionally slowing down or diverting in direction to catch a glimpse of what was happening behind. Eventually, she made her way back, waving the group to pick up speed, gesturing for Daniel to follow her as she caught up with Craig and Sava.

"Problem?" Craig said the moment she caught up.

"Orcs. There's a hunting party coming," Tula said. "At least thirty."

"Damn it. And the bird?"

"Still distracted."

"How far away are we?" Sava asked.

"Too far. But there's another exit," Tula said. "It's closer but harder to get to. More exposed to the raptors."

"Then we better move fast," Sava said, eyes narrowing in thought. A group of thirty Orcs catching them out in the open was dangerous, especially if they ended up fighting the raptors as well. In either case, there would be too many of them to block off entirely, forcing the Merchants to take part in the fight. If that happened, it was certain that there were going to be losses.

Tula nodded and sped up, taking the lead. At first, they ran in the same direction, but soon the group angled towards the cliff face, breaking through dense foliage. In short order, they came across a steep shale cliff. Nearly out of sight at the top of the shale cliff, they could see a small opening cut into the cliff face that was barely big enough for a single person.

Tula scrambled up the shale cliff, the broken rocks slipping and sliding beneath her feet. After ascending ten meters, she turned around, reaching for her bow as she waved the rest of the group onwards. The group had not waited for her, of course, and had started the ascent. But the treacherous shale rocks that threatened to dislodge under the slightest pressure made the entire journey harrowing.

As Daniel reached the bottom of the cliff, he frowned. The Healer looked up, eyeing the long ascent to the top and then at the slow, scrambling group. After a brief moment, he conjured his rope from his inventory and waved Asin over.

"Get the rest of the rope and tie it off at the top, as fast as you can," Daniel said. The Catkin's greater Agility and light bone structure meant she would be able to ascend with the least amount of trouble.

Asin nodded, waving down a couple of the other Adventurers and waving the rope in front of them as she jogged over. In short order, the Catkin had the rope from four other Adventurers stowed away in her inventory before she jogged to the side and then began her rapid ascent. The struggling Merchants and Adventurers could only glare at the young Catkin who scrambled up the unstable slope like it was firm earth beneath her.

"Good call," Craig said. "Daniel, we'll want you at the bottom if you don't mind. You, Omrak, Uppulu, Bjarne and I will hold the bottom. Hjalmar, Elisa, and Vivian will ascend with the Merchants and find suitable fighting positions. Rob, do you have any other of your traps?" Rob shook his head, and Craig sighed. "Then you need to go up too."

In short order, the team shook themselves out, getting ready for the Orcs. A tense ten minutes continued before Daniel heard the first signs of the incoming Orcs, the not subtle tramp of booted feet on the ground resounding through the gorge. As the Orcs finally made an appearance, their green skin and bulky tusked figures were more tattered and bedraggled than the Adventurers themselves. Not a single Orc was missing an injury—tears and still-bleeding wounds a testament of the kind of journey that they had. But, upon seeing the gathered expedition group, they roared in excitement, making those who were behind excited enough to join those ahead. At the sight, Daniel could only gulp and hold his weapon up, praying that the rest of his team could make their way up and provide some support.

***

The Orcs spread out before Daniel, snorting and growling as they worked up the nerve to attack. Daniel forcibly made himself relax, intent on catching the change in temperament, in mood just before the monsters would throw themselves forwards. He should not have bothered, for the signal to charge was not subtle at all. The leading Orc War Leader roared and swung his hand down before he threw himself forwards, intent on narrowing the gap between the pair. The Adventurers in turn crouched low, trying to work out the timing of rushing back to ensure they had sufficient momentum while not leaving the wall too far either.

As Daniel waited, his gaze flicked over the information presented to him, stopping first on the War Leader before moving onwards. A Level 2 Orc War Leader, a Level 9 War Raider, Level 4 Warrior, the numbers ranged significantly. It was surprising, though their health and Mana levels indicated that many of them including the War Leader were multi-classed. It was likely that those with low Levels had recently changed Classes—a testament to the needs of the tribe. That was good, since low Levels meant fewer combat-related Skills.

That was all that Daniel had time for, before the group was on them. Together, the Adventurers moved forwards, hunkering behind shields as they charged forwards, triggering Skills to absorb the rush. Just before the group met, arrows and spells fell, forcing the Orcs who had shields to raise them above their head, leaving them open for retaliatory attacks. As the Orcs stumbled, the Adventurers slammed into them, sending targeted opponents flying backwards.

Of course, being seriously outnumbered meant that each Adventurer was facing more than one Orc. The few polearm-wielding Adventurers were much safer, their longer weapons forcing their opponents to stutter their steps and dodge around the threatening weapons. For those without polearms, they could only hunker down and absorb the attacks on their armor.

Daniel grunted as a cut skipped off the rerebrace on his arm after impacting and denting the metal piece. He staggered to the side, cradling his injured arm that had lost feeling as he struggled to keep his weakened fingers around the haft of his weapon. Groaning, he staggered back, opening a space in their line as he desperately blocked more attacks with his shield and jerked his arm as he tried to get feeling back in. All around him, he could hear the grunts and clash of battle, the sudden addition of unwashed body and newly spilled blood filling his nostrils.

Another blow took his shield to the side, opening him up to a stab. Rather than backing off, Daniel threw himself forwards, feeling the blade skitter off the side of his chest plate as he grabbed his opponent around the edges of his collar and yanked them downwards and close. Turning, he spun the Orc with him, as he retreated, dragging the monster with him to block off others. Even as the Orc struggled to strike him with his sword, Daniel kept his hand tucked close to the other and jerked it around, sending the majority of the strikes skipping off his armor.

The moment his hand grew strong enough to grip the hammer properly, Daniel shoved the escaping Orc down one last time before triggering **Perrin's Blow** to smash his opponent into the ground. Even as he backed off to ensure the weakly struggling monster did not grab his legs, Daniel could see that the rest of the expedition group was not doing much better. Arrows from above were falling much less frequently, the Adventurers nearly out of projectiles. Only Vivian who had recovered her Mana could do much, and even then, the flaming arrows she sent down could only distract and disturb. In particular, of his friends, Daniel could see that Omrak was doing the worst, a particularly bad strike having torn open one of his thighs. The Northerner was badly off-balance and in front of the now-collapsed line, taking blows to his body constantly.

"Omrak!" Daniel cried out in surprise. The Healer shoved his shield in a feint as he began to pull together the spell formula to help his friend, cursing himself for forgetting to put himself next to his often-injured friend.

"Back!" Omrak roared.

Instinct told Daniel what the Northerner was about to do, but the other Adventurers did not move back. Rather than risk them, the Northerner threw himself forward into the middle of the Orc group, receiving another cut across his face for the risky action. In turn, he released the pent-up Rage, the red mist that collected around his body as each attack landed upon him with his Skill, the **Lightning's Call.** Arcs of electricity shot from his body, jumping from opponent to opponent, sending them falling backwards.

In the disruption, Sumuhan's maul crushed a head, Craig finished another stunned Orc, and Daniel finished his spell, sending a **Minor Healing II** towards his friend. Immediately, he began another spell.

"Switch!" Daniel called over to Bjarne who stood beside him. The halberd wielder swung his weapon one last time, injuring an opponent and stepping forwards and sideways as he forced a gap for Daniel to skitter around behind him. From above, a rain of arrows landed among the Orcs, taking advantage of their loose defences to injure and hurt as Omrak staggered back, bleeding from multiple wounds.

"I'm out!" Elisa called out.

"Me too!" Tula said.

"Go!" Craig answered even as he forced his way forwards to help guard Omrak. "Omrak, get back!"

"I can still fight!" the Northerner suited words to actions, beating apart a hasty block to sink his blade into the chest of an Orc. He moved to kick the Orc away, only to lose his balance slightly and lose his opportunity, his sword pulled out of his hands by the collapsing monster. As another Orc threatened him with an attack, Omrak had no choice but to back off.

"Idiot!" Daniel said, slapping his hand down on Omrak and transferring the **Healer's Mark** over before he yanked his friend off the front-line, the Orcs retreating a bit as they pulled their injured members off the front-line. "Drink a healing potion and go!"

Omrak grabbed his last healing potion, downing the drink before reaching sideways, withdrawing a shorter sword from his Inventory. "A Hero never abandons his friends!"

"Idiot!"

"Ropes!" Asin called out, having finally secured them. The Catkin began moving the ropes around, trying to ensure that the Merchants could grab hold of them as best she could. Once the

---

Merchants had a grip, their ascent sped up significantly.

"We need to break off," Daniel said as he twirled his hammer around his hand, focusing on another healing spell as the group backed up again, nearly to the edge of the cliff space.

"I'm open to ideas," Craig said.

"I…" Daniel's words were cut short as a screech from above drew all their attentions. The motion was instinctive, a leftover reaction from a time when humans and Orcs once lived in caves and feared the night and the monsters that existed beside them. The screech said it all, to their muted, civilized senses—something bigger, badder was coming.

From above, the mutated Nizhyne raptor fell, its wings tucked into its body as it targeted its prey. Beside it, smaller monsters flew, each of the smaller raptors the size of a large hound, the mutated raptor a monster that would make even a hippo quail. It dropped from the sky, seeking its prey. And, like prey the world over, they scattered and hunkered down, hoping they were not the ones to be picked.

Too late, the stooping raptor caught its prey, lifting one of the Merchant's into the air. It flapped its wings, carrying the Merchant and his bags with it as it flew upwards, taking the man into the sky, his chest pierced by talons the size of Daniel's forearms. Already, it circled upwards, the smaller raptors, brave in the presence of their larger brother attacking and tearing at Merchants, Adventurers, and Orcs in turn before they too departed.

"Move!" Daniel said as he finished shoving the raptor aside. He empowered his foot, sending **Perrin's Blow** into a startled Orc before he waved the rest of the Adventurers up. "Let's go!"

The Adventurers reacted first, turning and running for the slope and reaching for the ropes. Above them, Vivian and Rob threw the last of their magic spells, distracting and harrying their pursuit as the Adventurers scrambled up the slope. Under Daniel's fingers, the coarse rope danced and twisted as those before him climbed, his feet slipping on the loose shale. Clouds of choking dust floated up, making him cough as he swarmed up the rope. Once upon a time, Daniel knew, he had had some skill at climbing. Portions of that skill, that knowledge, still lay within him, broken memories of hanging off ropes, squirming down the wet cord as water splashed on his face. Of shoving himself against rocks to squirm upwards. A memory. Broken and shattered, by his Gift.

Daniel shook his head, driving the thoughts away as he focused on the climb. Now was not the time, not with angry Orcs that had recovered beneath and Merchants above. The strong Adventurer swarmed up the rope, using his strength to pull himself up bodily and found that he soon had overtaken the last Merchant in line.

From above, the other ranged Adventurers had taken to throwing rocks down the slope, shards of broken rock skipping and slamming down on the crawling Orcs.

"Raptors!"

The cry from above had Daniel turning around, bringing his shield to bear. He snarled as he saw that the Mutated Raptor had discarded its gory prey at some point and was now coming back, intent on finishing off the rest of the expedition. As it neared, Daniel ran through his options. He had no ranged weaponry, no spells that could hurt the monster. No way to distract it.

"Don't!" Daniel said as he turned to Omrak. The Northerner, eyes intent on the incoming flock relaxed, shooting a glance at Daniel who shook his head again, all the while forming a healing spell in his mind. The Northerner was wrapped in red, a pale reddish-pink mist across his body as the injuries he had sustained and still bled from fueled his Rage. It gave Omrak strength and allowed him to ignore the damage and even lessened the damage he received, but it did nothing to alleviate the damage he already carried. The Northerner could not take another beating, even Daniel's repeated healing was barely doing anything more than keeping the man alive and moving.

As the raptors began their final descent, another of their party acted. Tula stood up from above, swinging her arms and tossing small, frayed pouches down the slope. They struck the ground and the rocks and Orcs below, spreading their fetid and slimy contents. Daniel could swear he saw the way the mutated raptor's eyes shifted, its attention drawn to the new source of smell, to its prey. As quick as a thought, the creature shifted its trajectory, its counterparts following suit.

The Orcs bellowed in anger and surprise at the smelly attack, the War Leader looking upwards and then raising his hand and releasing another shout. This one froze everyone, the raptors on their final descent freezing or twisting away as the Skill took effect. Even the Merchants and Adventurers froze, their bodies locking up under the Skill's assault.

Some of the raptors including the mutated Nizhnye raptor managed to shake the Skill off, but they were too close to the ground and were forced to land with flared wings. The Orcs, angered by the assault, switched their attention, launching strikes using Skills or just reaching over to smash the grounded birds. A few of the flock never managed to shake the Skill off in time, slamming into the ground at full speed and expiring. As for the rest, they circled upwards, beating their wings as they took to the air for another assault.

"Thank Erlis," Prek said as the majority of the raptors landed below them. Daniel, crouched next to him with his shield ready to deflect the monsters, looked over and truly saw the Merchant for once. "I thought I'd never get to fish again."

"Fish…" Daniel's eyes widened, turning to look down. Beneath them, the Orcs had received another group of reinforcements while the mutated raptor swung its beak, pushing its attackers back as it got ready to fly away.

"Quickly. Release your boat," Daniel said, gesturing down at the group below.

"What?" Prek said.

"Drop your boat on the raptor. If we can injure it, it'll be forced to fight the Orcs," Daniel said. "It'll give us time to run."

"But my boat…"

"Do it!" Daniel snapped, glaring at the Merchant. Prek gulped and raised his hand, calling forth his Skill and the boat that was stored away. A hole appeared and from it, the boat appeared, falling onto the ground. Under the weight of the wooden vessel, the unsteady shale slipped, tumbling down along with the vessel itself. The wooden vessel rumbled down the slope, throwing up shards of rock and dust as it fell. The nimbler Orcs threw themselves aside but the mutated raptor, hopping on its clawed feet, could barely get away before it struck a wing, cracking bone and throwing the monster to the ground. As it struck the ground and the monster, the boat finally gave way, the wooden decking splitting apart and sending splinters and wooden shards everywhere.

"Good job!" Craig called out and then waved his hand. "Now, get moving!"

Prek moaned, seeing the shattered remnants of his boat.

"Come on. I'm sure Sava will buy you a new one," Daniel said, shoving Prek's shoulder. The Merchant let out another low moan, but he took to the ropes, scurrying up the cliff. Behind him, Daniel took one last look below him as the Orcs and raptors fought, entangled in a skirmish that neither one could fully break away from.

***

"Daniel!" Tula grabbed the Healer's arm as he came up the rope, and the remaining Adventurers retrieved the remaining climbing aids and helped the Merchants to recover their energy. Beneath, the fight between the Orcs and the mutated raptor was coming to an end, the overwhelming numbers of the Orcs having won the day. However, beneath the feet of the raptor, numerous corpses lay, a testament to the strength and savagery of the creature.

"Yes?" Daniel said, following along behind Tula. She brought him over to the small entrance that the Merchants and Adventurers were squeezing through, pointing at the low slope between and Sava who stood there.

"You were a Miner before, were you not?" Sava said.

"You want me to break down the walls?" Daniel said, catching on almost immediately. He turned his head, regarding the stone and then shook his head. "I don't have a pickaxe. And this is granite. If I had Mining Skills…"

"You don't?" Sava said frowning.

"Never took them," Daniel said. After all, a Skill that broke more rock or located cracks in stone for optimal strikes might be useful for a Miner but would be useless for him as an Adventurer. Or so, Daniel had thought. Now, he was reconsidering.

"Out of the way!" snapped one of the Merchants as he pushed past, entering the small tunnel.

"Damn," Sava's lips pressed together and then he shook his head. "I guess I'll have to use it."

"Use it?" Tula said, eyes narrowing.

In reply, Sava took out his pouch a simple-looking clay block, one that was filled with runes. Tula gasped while Daniel just looked puzzled.

"It's a temporary abode enchantment," Sava said. "It'll create a clay tent. Useful for when the weather turns very bad."

Daniel looked between Sava and the entrance, then at the struggling Adventurers who streamed past and nodded. At Sava's gesture, Tula and he entered, leaving Sava to bring up the rear. In short order, they were about ten feet in and the Merchant had turned around, placing the enchantment on the ground and triggering it. He then hurried back, waving the inquisitive Daniel back as well.

At first, the enchanted block glowed, then it began to grow. Slowly at first, small shifts, then they exploded in size. First, it doubled, then doubled again, then it gained in size at an ever-increasing rate. The small gap between the walls in the cliff were soon filled, the magically enchanted walls of the clay block forming and shattering as they came into contact with the unyielding edges. Once empty space filled as stone cracked and grew, filling the gap between the walls as the magic continued to play out even when the initial enchantment was broken. In seconds, the enchanted clay was five feet tall and it kept growing, filling the space and moving towards the watching pair.

"When is it supposed to stop?" Daniel said, backing off slowly as he eyed the still-growing blockage.

"I… don't know," Sava replied.

Another crack, and the clay plug bulged again. The clay grew explosively, nearly taking up half the space they had left. Jaw dropping, Daniel turned Sava around and shouted, "RUN!"

Behind them, the creaking and groaning of pressurised enchanted clay and granite resounded as the pair beat a hasty retreat, waving the rest of the team onwards. At least, Daniel thought as he ran for his life, the gap had been thoroughly plugged.

Epilogue

Two weeks later, the group stumbled into the village where they had set the expedition wagons. Tired, weary, but with no other losses, the Merchants and Adventurers collapsed in exhaustion. The few guards and villagers took action, helping the tired and worn expedition to rest and heal. Even if Daniel had used his Mana and Gift to care for the team, constant healing and fixing left its own scars and a wearied mind and body.

No further signs of the Orcs had appeared. Whether they had lost the clan or the clan had taken so much damage that they had to break off, the expedition were no longer bothered by the Orcs. On the other hand, Sava and Craig had refused to slow the expedition down, keeping them moving at a good pace for the better part of a week before exhaustion had finally forced a pause.

At the camp, Tula broke off to report to the older Ranger while the rest of the team relaxed, many falling asleep the moment they made their way into the tents and other temporary accommodation provided for them. As for Daniel, he took a seat by the campfire, liberal use of his Gift allowing the Healer to stay up. Seated by the village center's campfire where a cook had placed a roast, Daniel stared at the fire until Asin dropped down beside him, resting her light form against the healer.

"That was interesting," Daniel said to his oldest friend.

Asin purred in answer, eyelids drooping.

"Think she'll leave us?" Daniel said, looking to where the Ranger had disappeared to.

Asin shrugged but then roused herself enough to add, "Dungeon better."

"For us, maybe. This… this is her world, isn't it?" Daniel said as he reflected on the past few weeks. Never mind their bad luck in running into the Orcs, the young Ranger had been correct. Expeditions always ran a chance of something bad happening. If not for the Ranger's knowledge of the surroundings, understanding of the monsters, and her bravery, none of them would have made their way back. Sure, there were a number of close calls. And they had lost some of the Merchants. But…

But it was clear, at least to Daniel, that this was where the youngster really did excel. Not the Dungeon, but out here, where monsters and Orcs, where dangers grew wild and uncontrolled. And, as for them…

"I think I like the Dungeons better too," Daniel said finally.

Asin snorted in amusement, and Daniel turned—only to realise that the snort was actually a snore. He stared at his little Catkin friend leaning against him and chuckled, content to let her sleep. They were safe. And soon, they would be back, running Dungeons.

Author's Note

If you enjoyed reading the book, please do leave a review and rating. Not only is it a big ego boost, it also helps sales and convinces me to write more in the series!

If you enjoyed this, check out my other series:
-       Life in the North (An Apocalyptic LitRPG)
https://readerlinks.com/l/729295
-       A Gamer's Wish (An Urban Fantasy LitRPG)
https://readerlinks.com/l/729151
-       A Thousand Li (a cultivation series inspired by Chinese wuxia and xianxia novels)
https://readerlinks.com/l/729231

For more great information about LitRPG series, check out the Facebook groups:
   - Gamelit Society
https://www.facebook.com/groups/LitRPGsociety/
   - LitRPG Books
https://www.facebook.com/groups/LitRPG.books/

About the Author

Tao Wong is an avid fantasy and sci-fi reader who spends his time working and writing in the North of Canada. He's spent way too many years doing martial arts of many forms and having broken himself too often, now spends his time writing about fantasy worlds.

If you'd like to support him directly, Tao now has a Patreon page where previews of all his new books can be found!
https://www.patreon.com/taowong

For updates on the series and the author's other books (and special one-shot stories), please visit his website: http://www.mylifemytao.com

Subscribers to Tao's mailing list will receive exclusive access to short stories in the Thousand Li and System Apocalypse universes:
https://www.subscribepage.com/taowong

Or visit his Facebook Page:
https://www.facebook.com/taowongauthor

About the Publisher

Starlit Publishing is wholly owned and operated by Tao Wong. It is a science fiction and fantasy publisher focused on the LitRPG & cultivation genres. Their focus is on promoting new, upcoming authors in the genre whose writing challenges the existing stereotypes while giving a rip-roaring good read.

For more information on Starlit Publishing, visit our website!
https://www.starlitpublishing.com/

You can also join Starlit Publishing's mailing list to learn of new, exciting authors and book releases.
https://starlitpublishing.com/newsletter-signup/

www.ingramcontent.com/pod-product-compliance
Lightning Source LLC
Chambersburg PA
CBHW070457200726
48293CB00007B/2257